FINDING
ABBEY
ROAD

An **EXILE**
Novel

Kevin Emerson

KATHERINE TEGEN BOOKS
An Imprint of HarperCollins Publishers

Map art © 2016 by Jaime Temairik
Photos by Kevin Emerson

Katherine Tegen Books is an imprint of HarperCollins Publishers.

Finding Abbey Road: An Exile Novel

 PC STUDIO

Library of Congress Cataloging-in-Publication Data

Names: Emerson, Kevin, author.
Title: Finding Abbey Road : an Exile novel / Kevin Emerson.
Description: First edition. | New York, NY : Katherine Tegen Books, an imprint of
    HarperCollinsPublishers, [2016] | Summary: Torn between wanting to stay with her
    band Dangerheart and her soulmate Caleb, and taking off in a different direction at her
    dream college, Summer travels to London, with Caleb, to unlock the missing songs
    mystery, but the last clues present an impossible challenge.
Identifiers: LCCN 2015029198 | ISBN 9780062134011 (hardback)
Subjects: | CYAC: Rock groups—Fiction. | Bands (Music)—Fiction. | Love—Fiction.
    | College choice—Fiction | London (England)—Fiction. | England—Fiction.
    | BISAC: JUVENILE FICTION / Social Issues / Dating & Sex. | JUVENILE
    FICTION / Performing Arts / Music. | JUVENILE FICTION / Family / Siblings.
Classification: LCC PZ7.E5853 Fi 2016 | DDC [Fic]—dc23 LC record available at http://
    lccn.loc.gov/2015029198

Typography by Carla Weise
16 17 18 19 20   CG/RRDH   10 9 8 7 6 5 4 3 2 1
❖
First Edition

To the exiles . . .

THE FAMILY ECLIPT

MELANIE FOWLER
Val's mom

RANDY
*Caleb's uncle,
Eli's old band mate*

CHARITY
Caleb's mom

THE POPARTS PLANE

ETHAN MYERS
*Postcards from Ariel singer,
Summer's ex*

KELLEN McHUGH
*Allegiance bassist,
knows about tapes!*

JASON FLETCHER
*Candy Shell Records,
signed Ethan*

MILES ELLISON
Allegiance guitarist

THE
ALLEGIANCE
CLUSTER

*All Hail
Minions!*

PARKER FRANCIS
Allegiance drummer

JERROD FLETCHER
*Head of Candy Shell,
former Allegiance manager*

*Supreme
Commander*

*The
Unfortunatelys*

MAYA BARNES
*Dating Matt,
Summer's friend,
Candy Shell Intern*

Bait

*Fluffy Poodle and
the #s of Doom!*

THE ASTEROID
BELT OF BANDS

Freak   *Show*

Finding Abbey Road

THE FUTURE?

Encore to an Empty Room

College Applications:
Due soon!

MATT
Drummer

JON
Guitarist

THE DANGERHEART GALAXY

VAL
Bassist
Runaway

SUMMER
Manager

- - Siblings! - -

CALEB
Singer

- - 3 months! - -

Lost songs

ELI WHITE
Caleb & Val's dad,
Allegiance singer
Died 1998

CARLSON SQUARED
Summer's parents

EXILE

Part 1:
Monday

10:18 a.m.

I hold my breath.

Don't dare say more.

Stopping time with my lungs.

Afraid of what comes next.

Beyond our safe place in the shadow of a metal sun, the universe continues to expand. There are some galaxies so far from us, heading in the opposite direction, that we will never see their light. Whole parts of the universe we will never even glimpse. There is also an entire galaxy on a collision course with ours.

All of this is beyond us. There is so much we'll never even know. So little we can control.

"Fuck," says Caleb quietly. He flips the navy blue guitar pick between his fingers. Its gold lettering catches the light reflecting off the sun.

3

Regent Sounds.

A guitar shop in London.

A pick dropped on the floor in a basement club in New York City, three days ago. Dropped when its owner fled the scene. It's been in my pocket, a burning secret, since then.

Caleb's breakfast burrito sits on the grass between us, half-eaten. I should have let him eat a little more before I told him. If I were him, and I just got this news, it would be the end of food for the day. He tears off a corner of the foil wrapping and balls it up between his fingers. Shoots it out onto the sidewalk. It spins out sunlight like a disco ball, a tiny falling star.

A far comet.

I allow myself to exhale. Risk taking his hand. He's going to freak out, any second now. . . . And he has every right to.

It's not every morning that you find out your long-dead father is actually alive.

I try to keep from asking dumb questions.

Are you okay? Of course he's not.

What are you thinking? A million things, obviously.

Caleb stares into the distance between us. He seems stuck, like his brain is overloaded, too many thoughts at once, the little wheel spinning. I see his chest moving, rapid breaths, his lovely eyes flicking, eyelids battered by storm clouds.

Finally, his thumb starts to rub the back of my hand.

"Tell me again."

"Your dad is alive," I say. "Eli . . . is in London. I don't know how. But I saw him."

Caleb nods. He sits there frozen for another few seconds and then those dark eyes find me. "Thank you."

"For what? Ruining your day, your year—"

He manages a sort-of smile. "All that was already ruined. Thank you for telling me."

I lean over and wrap my arms around him. "I'm so sorry." I feel him collapse against my shoulder. I can't even imagine what this is like for him. I kiss him gently, then harder. . . . In spite of everything, his lips are as soft as ever and I want him to know that I am here for him, right now, that we are unbreakable, a perfect fit. . . .

But after a second, he pulls back. "It's okay. Actually . . . it's fine."

"Tell me."

He sighs. "I don't know, it's like, all my life I've been living with this weird ghost. It was right in the corner of my eye, but I couldn't quite see it. When I found out Eli's identity, and the ghost got a name, a face, and a past, that just made it worse. The emptiness I used to feel became this hole. . . . And now? I don't even know. A part of me always hoped he might be alive, might be out there somewhere, even though I knew that was impossible. I never wanted to admit that. I knew it was stupid . . ."

"Not stupid. And, apparently not impossible."

"I wish I'd seen him."

"I wish you had, too," I say. "If Jason hadn't shown up . . ."

This is the part that kills me the most. So many things happened last Friday night in New York. The whole day had already been crazy enough: We followed a note from Eli White that led us to his old guitar at the Hard Rock Cafe. We thought we'd find his third lost song there, but the guitar was empty . . . and then Jon defected to join stupid Ethan Myers's band, Postcards from Ariel, and Val's mom and boyfriend showed up at the gig, and Matt got punched and Val ran off and pretty much everything was shattered.

Caleb went after Val. Randy took Matt to the hospital, and so I was alone when the mysterious texts started coming in, pointing me toward a club called Ten Below Zero, with the promise of finding Eli's final song. Time was short. I took off without waiting. . . .

Typical Summer. If I had just waited for Caleb, we could have gotten to Ten Below together, both seen Eli White alive and onstage, and Caleb could have met his father . . .

Or maybe if I waited it would have been too late, and he would have already been gone. There was so little time.

So instead, it was just me. Watching Eli White as he sat on stage, hunched over a guitar, playing a song from beyond the grave. And then Jason Fletcher showed up, and Eli pulled his vanishing act before he could be recognized by anyone but me.

For three days I've been carrying this secret, wondering what to do with it, whether it would hurt Caleb more or less if he knew the truth.

But he was already hurt.

He deserved to know.

We crossed the country, risked our band and our futures, probably lost both. Sure, we have two of Eli's three lost songs, but that no longer feels nearly as important as the fact that we almost had *him*. And all we have left now is a location:

London.

That's where Eli is. At least, I'm pretty sure.

"So," says Caleb, "now what?"

As always, that is the question.

"I don't know," I say. "Go back to fourth period?" It feels so lame. Here we are, outside the bounds of time and space. It's hard to even remember that it's just a Monday in February and we are supposed to be in class. How can we possibly just go back to everything as usual?

Caleb smiles, but only for a second. Then he's dead serious again. "We have to find him."

I get out my phone. "I'll try our mystery lead again. . . ."

I send a text to that same phone number that led me to Eli. The same unknown person who delivered Eli's old guitar case to Caleb's door on Christmas Day.

Summer: Caleb knows. We want to get in touch with Eli.

"How did he do it?" Caleb wonders. He picks up his

burrito, takes a halfhearted bite, then drops it on the grass again.

"You mean Eli? How'd he fake his death? I have no idea."

That's been eating at me, too. It seems like kind of a massively huge deal to erase yourself like Eli did. Like something you'd need help to pull off. Not just actually faking a drowning, but connections to get out of the country, money . . . all that cinematic stuff.

"I went back to the Wikipedia page," I say. "There's no mention of whether Eli's body was ever found. I always just assumed it was, or there would have been a story there. The article in the *LA Times* from when it happened says that his wallet was found on the Santa Monica pier, his car was in the lot, and his shirt was found washed ashore a few miles down the beach the next morning. At that time the search was still ongoing. But then there's never any mention of a body."

My phone buzzes:

(424) 828-3710: That's not possible. I'm sorry. Too risky.

I show the text to Caleb.

He laughs and stares into the grass, the computer overloaded again, but then he nods to himself. "Tell whoever that is that if he doesn't help us, we're going public with the songs, and about Eli being alive, all of it. We'll call CNN or *Rolling Stone* or whoever will listen."

It lifts my spirits to hear him say this. To want to fight.

But I still have to ask: "Would you really want to do that?"

Caleb shrugs. "Why not? He owes us, doesn't he? Don't I have the right to talk to my own father, who's been avoiding me my whole life?"

I kiss him. "Yes, you do."

"So then if he won't make the choice, we'll make it for him. Don't you think?"

"Definitely."

Summer: If you don't help us, we're going public with everything.

(424) 828-3710: Aren't you supposed to be in class right now?

Summer: Not a priority today.

(424) 828-3710: Are you even at school?

Summer: We're serious. Please help us.

. . .

"What's he saying?" Caleb asks. He's taken out his phone and started texting. I want to ask who with, but I resist. I don't want to be the girlfriend who's in every inch of his business (even though I want to be), especially not today.

"Waiting . . ."

(424) 828-3710: Ok listen: go to the athletics hall at school. Trophy case by the gym doors. Bottom left corner. See what you find. I'll be in touch shortly.

"Weird." I hold out the phone so Caleb can read. He doesn't look up for a second, still finishing a text, and I fight another urge to know who with.

Then he reads my phone. "What does that mean?"

"I don't know," I say.

"Well, let's go," says Caleb, standing. "We can't stay here all day, and there is no way I'm going to sit through my classes."

We stand and leave our oasis beneath the metal sun, the spot where Caleb first told me about Eli. We pass the spot on the sidewalk where I first kissed him, which seemed so obvious in the moment and crazy in hindsight and like two years ago now.

Every step feels odd. A little dizzy. Like, who knows where we are heading now?

I finish my burrito as we walk. It's a warm day even for LA in February, sweat between my shoulder blades and behind my knees. Part of me misses that biting cold in Chicago and New York last week, being wrapped in layers. Or maybe I miss being wrapped in certainty. There was something about that road trip. We had purpose, a mission. We were off the grid, space travelers with velocity. Now we're back and I feel adrift and exposed.

When I throw away my wrapper, Caleb tosses out the rest of his burrito. He shoves his hands in his pockets. I reach for his arm, holding him by the elbow. He is still distant, shell-shocked. I want him back, present, arm around me, a kiss even, but of course he's withdrawn. I try to imagine what it would be like to have your world change so much in these singular bursts, all over the course of six months:

Your mom sitting you down and revealing who your dad actually was . . .

Your dad speaking to you through tapes from beyond the grave . . .

Finding out that grave is actually empty.

10:41 a.m.

We walk silently back through the mall toward school. Everyone seems fake to me today: moms in their yoga pants with their expensive strollers; business types in their crisp folds talking at full volume into earpieces like they are the most important objects in the universe. I want to lash out at them and tell them, Wake up! Not everybody is living in your little bubble of self-satisfaction. Not everything is so perfect.

But maybe I'm just feeling wounded.

The moment I got back from New York City I was grounded for the lies surrounding my Stanford interview. That's a whole other thing. I was offered an interview and ditched it, telling my parents that it actually happened. Who does that? Me, apparently. Which leads me to wonder who exactly I am these days. The two versions, who I want to be versus who my parents want me to be, feeling more and more different.

Of course the interview ended up working out, through

no fault of my own. The interviewer, Andre, called my house when another available time came up, only I was on the way to New York when he called. Whoops. I guess I could have defied my parents further, refused to fly home when they caught me . . . but then what? It would be kind of ridiculous to run away, to live like Val. Compared to her life, I should probably be whistling happily along. So how come I don't feel that way?

Since I got back, I've been feeling furious at my parents and the interview, even mocking Andre with his list of questions.

"How do you picture yourself impacting the Stanford campus?"

Like a success supernova!

Like an android my parents built.

Like brooding dark matter . . .

Actually he was a pretty cool guy. And side note: I probably nailed the interview. I might well be this strange and precious *"Stanford material"* that Dad dreams about, in spite of myself.

And then when I'm not feeling angry, I'm racked with guilt: for letting down my parents, for lying and being irresponsible, even though I don't actually believe in the very expectations that I'm supposedly *not* living up to.

Sometimes I feel like I'm not their Catherine at all anymore. But is Summer a liar, a coward? I feel like if I was somehow a better version of me, I could be both. I don't know why I can't pull off being what they want and also what I want. Maybe some stronger version of me could make my parents see the value in *my* version, the value in Summer and her dreams, without having to lie, to hide myself from them.

Maybe I could have been more honest with them this winter, this whole last year, not just about my interview, but also my uncertainty about what I really want to do next year. I could have really put it on the table for them and explained why managing Dangerheart is so important to me.

But I also know my parents. They don't make it quite that easy. Then again, have I ever given them the chance?

It doesn't help that the future of Summer hinges on a band that is currently scattered in fragments. Caleb and Matt are the only members who are even at school today. Jon is getting home this afternoon, according to his posts, but he played two more shows with Postcards from Ariel and is flying back with them. I'm not sure he could even be called a band member at this point.

And worst of all, we still have no idea where Val is. I know Caleb and Charity have tried getting in touch with her. I've sent texts to no reply. I keep thinking she'll resurface, if for no other reason than she knows Jason Fletcher, the scout at Candy Shell Records, is expecting an answer from us today. He offered us a huge record deal, on one condition: we turn over the tapes of Eli's lost songs. Can we possibly do that?

It's the half-million dollar question. And Val was counting on that money more than the rest of us, to pay for her legal fees as she pursues emancipation from her crazy mother, to rent an apartment of her own. . . .

But I'm not sure how your band can sign a record deal when you don't have a band.

Would Stanford really be so bad for Summer?

Oh hell, I don't know what to do about any of it.

"Hold on." Caleb stops us at the edge of the parking lot.

School is between periods. We watch from a distance as students stream from one door to another. Everyone talking, laughing, silent, or joking, all deep in the drama of their lives, all connected by classes, late bells, hunger pangs, the desire to fit in, to stand out, to be the star of their movie.

We all think we're the sun at the center of our universe.

Of course the center of the universe is actually an all-consuming black hole. Does that mean that our best-case scenario is that we're each a tiny solar system, with a handful of planets, born to burn for only a cosmic blink of an eye, one of trillions that have shined before and after?

Maybe.

And yet still they all hurry, darting up the steps, getting to class, cramming for the quiz, rushing over to the Armpit to quickly suck down a cigarette, rushing to the wall behind the gym for a quick feel-up . . . all of them unaware that from this distance they are little more than ants on parade.

14

But then what does that make Caleb and me?

Out of the flow, apart from the parade, spectators. Does that make us blessed or cursed? Are we more awake, more aware, or just hopelessly lost in space?

Is there someone watching us from a similar distance?

Oh my God, Summer, get a grip.

"You okay?" Caleb asks.

"Fine," I say, shaking it off. "I'm the one who should be asking you that."

"It's all right," he says, like it mostly isn't.

The second passing bell rings. The last stragglers stamp out their cigarettes, adjust their bras and boners, stow away their cheat sheets, and sprint for the doors.

Then the building is still again.

We cross the parking lot and enter through the glass doors of the PopArts wing. We skirt quickly by open classroom doors, until we are in the window-lined hallway that rounds the back of the auditorium.

"Aw, man," says Caleb, "I just remembered there's a quiz in amplifier physics."

"Should you go?" I ask him.

Caleb shakes his head, allows almost a glimpse of a smile. "Pretty sure this is more important."

The hall ends and we duck through old blue double doors into the athletics wing, a bleak, windowless hall of faded tan brick walls and stained brown tile floors, reeking of sweat and ever-damp showers.

15

The walls are lined with sad trophy cases. Most of the photos and trophies are at least ten years old, some older than that. Once Mount Hope became famous for PopArts, any kid with real athletic prowess went elsewhere.

We find the case beside the gym doors.

It's for the swim team.

It's as dusty as the others. Photo corners have curled away from the foil paper background, its shine dulled with time. Some of the medals that hung beside pictures lie on the bottom of the case.

We look over the items. Apparently Mount Hope had state champion swimmers in the 1980s, and one kid named Topher went to Nationals and even swam in the Junior Olympics.

"There." Caleb points to the bottom corner: a photo of four boys standing in their Speedos, arms around each other. They are grinning and holding up the silver medals around their necks. A strip of paper beneath the photo reads:

Countywide JV Invitational 1991. 200m Medley Relay 2nd Place

There are no names on the paper, but he's easy to spot: Eli White, second from the left, smiling brightly and actually looking better in a Speedo than his later, skinny-rock-star appearance would suggest. Actually, he's got kind of great shoulders, which I tell myself not to think and definitely not to say because eww that's my boyfriend's dad.

But more importantly, he looks so young, and that smile: it's got a light that I can't ever remember seeing in his later photos.

"Did you know about this?" I ask Caleb.

He shakes his head. "I don't think anyone did. He was only a freshman then."

"When did he and Randy meet?" I wonder.

"I think when Eli was a junior?"

"This photo is ten years before Eli died. I guess if he stopped swimming after freshman year, and never did varsity, maybe no one ever made the connection."

That said, here is another piece of information that seems to be conveniently missing from the narrative about Eli's death.

I text our mystery informant.

Summer: We're looking at the photo. So Eli was a good swimmer.

(424) 828-3710: A very good swimmer.

Summer: We already know he didn't actually drown. We need more.

. . .

(424) 828-3710: When can you meet?

I show Caleb the message. "My calendar is pretty free at this point," he says.

Summer: Whenever.

. . .

(424) 828-3710: My associate will pick you up in twenty

17

minutes. By the loading docks behind school.

The message makes an arctic chill pass through my abdomen.

"You up for this?" I ask Caleb.

I wonder if I am.

He just shrugs. "Does it matter?"

Summer: We'll be there.

10:58 a.m.

We kill time in the Green Room. Coach says hello and looks at us sideways, no doubt wondering why we're not in class. But he doesn't hassle us.

There's no one manning the espresso stand during this period but there is a self-serve pot of coffee. Caleb and I fill cups, then see that there's no milk or sugar out. We drink them black and bitter.

It fits.

We stand around, fidgeting and quiet, try hugging, but we're wound too tight.

After fifteen minutes we head out the back hallway, past the practice spaces, down the stairs, and out. A hot breeze lashes our faces, funneled between the high school and the community center next door, carrying the smell of the Dumpsters that sit just beyond a low concrete wall. . . .

Suddenly it is September again—either five months or five years or five centuries ago, it's hard to tell—and

Caleb is playing a concert to no one, standing on this very wall, until I startle him. It's intense to remember that super-charged moment. Everything new, every moment a first, full of possibility and magic . . .

It's so different from now, when the world feels hollow and mocking. That September afternoon seems so inno-cent. Maybe this is how it always is. Like it's only when you look back that can you see how much you didn't know, see what a silly dreamer you were.

But, no, we weren't wrong to dream, because it turned out we were right! More right than we knew. We dreamed of a band and that happened, a *great* band. We dreamed of finding Eli, of making Caleb's past whole. We did that, too. And it's because of all that we *did* do that we're here now, with so much further to go.

Deep breath, Summer. Let the caffeine sink in.

Caleb puts his arm around me. "I can't believe you found me here that day." I'm glad to know he's thinking the same thing. "I never would have come this far without you."

I resist the urge to question how far we've really come, given that we're standing right back where we started and our band is in shambles. Our life in orbit around the Dump-sters.

But no, I have to believe we're headed somewhere. And he's right: we knew enough to believe in each other. At least I'm sure of that. We may be back where we started, but we have come too far, way too far, to let our doubts win.

"We did it together," I say, and turn him toward me and kiss him, harder than he's ready for. It takes him a second to respond, but then he does, and for one brief moment we both remember that there is also just this, *us*, kisses like comfort, and a heat that starts to build each second that our mouths and tongues and bodies are in contact—

A car engine roars from around the corner.

We pull apart. Let the world back in.

Damn.

"Are you ready for whatever's next?" Caleb asks me.

"No idea. You?"

"No idea."

11:12 a.m.

The car rounds the corner with a squeal of tires. It's a cherry-red Audi. I recognize it before it pulls to a stop and I see who's inside.

"Guys." Ari Fletcher lowers his expensive silver sunglasses. He's a senior who still looks like he's made of potatoes, and still has his obnoxious giant red headphones around his neck, but today, his standard-issue, know-it-all smirk is gone.

Actually, he looks scared as hell.

"Come on," he says. "Get in, already."

"Huh?" I can't help saying, because if Ari is here, then that means . . .

In my mind, I feel big heavy puzzle pieces sliding into place.

"I'm supposed to drive you," he says, checking the clock. "We have to hurry."

"Where are we going?" Caleb asks.

Ari checks his phone. He swallows hard and glances around like we're in a spy movie. "He won't tell me. Just that if I don't bring you, I'm grounded for a month and I can't go to Cabo for spring break, so get in."

"Who's *he*?" I ask but I don't really need to.

I'm pretty sure I know.

11:14 a.m.

Caleb slides in the backseat. I take shotgun. Before I sit, Ari brushes a pile off the seat: takeout cups, energy bar wrappers, drumsticks, comic books, a copy of *Pump It!* magazine. His car smells like chocolate and boy. The second I close the door he tears off down the alley.

"So," I say, "let me guess: Jason is behind all this." I'm not even sure how that could be possible but who else could it be? There's no one who's been more invested in messing with us—

But Ari laughs dismissively. "Yeah right." He revs the gas as we sit at the stoplight outside school, then guns it out onto Main Street, our necks whiplashing. "Like I'd do this for *him*."

21

"Then who?" Caleb asks.

Ari is about to reply when his phone utters a sensual female moan.

"Nice," I mutter.

Ari picks it up and reads a text. "One sec, gonna let him know that we're on the way . . ."

He replies with his thumb while drifting back and forth in our lane. "Ari . . . ," I say as we race up on a line of cars stopped at a red light. I grab the wheel to get his attention.

"I got it," he says, glancing up and slamming the brakes.

His phone coos as his message sends.

"Are you going to tell us where we're going, or who is behind this?" I ask.

Ari just stares ahead at the traffic, his face tight. Then his phone moans again.

"Ugh, can you please silence that?"

"I'll put it on vibrate," he says. He might mean that as a joke, but his delivery is halfhearted. He checks the text and holds it up so we can both see the sender and the message:

Dad: Santa Monica pier.

"Your dad . . . ," I say.

"Jerrod Fletcher?" Caleb asks from the back.

"I don't get why he wants to talk to *you*," says Ari. "Does this have something to do with your label offer? Cuz believe me, I can understand why you'd be hesitant to work with my brother. He's kind of a d-bag sometimes and—"

"Yeah," I say quickly, glancing at Caleb as I do. "That's basically it. We're not sure whether or not we want to work with Jason." If that's what Ari is most inclined to believe, we'll go with that.

"It's huge money," says Ari. He sounds jealous.

"It is," says Caleb, "and we were supposed to give him an answer by today . . . I guess your dad wants to talk it over, try to persuade us or something."

"Whoo, yeah," says Ari. "I'm glad I'm just dropping you off and don't actually have to be there. He gets pretty pissy about stuff like this."

"Thanks for the warning," I say.

Meanwhile, my midsection is doing backflips into a pool of adrenaline.

Jerrod Fletcher is the one who led me to Eli . . .

Who sent Caleb the guitar case.

Which means Jerrod Fletcher knows Eli is alive.

Has known for sixteen years . . .

Does anyone else? We met Kellen McHugh, Eli's old band mate. He seemed to have no idea. I'm pretty sure Jason has no clue. Neither does Caleb's uncle, Randy. I always just assumed Jerrod was part of the enemy team after Eli's songs. . . .

But maybe he is something else entirely.

I try to catch Caleb's eye again. I want to break this down with him so badly, but once more his gaze is buried in his phone. God, who is he texting now? I know I shouldn't stick my nose in, but I have to say something. I'll try to keep it casual.

Summer: What's up?

Caleb: Nothing.

My thumbs twitch, wanting more.

Summer: Let's not tell Ari anything we don't have to.

Caleb: Agreed.

But other than swearing at the traffic on the 405, Ari doesn't feel like talking, either. He drives like an idiot, or he's just really nervous, weaving in and out of lanes, gunning the engine, and yet never quite improving his position on the choked highway. After a few miles, he puts on Silent-Noize, a rap metal band whose goal is to pump up jocks before they cause bodily harm, or to make you break speed limits. We all sit there in silence.

Eventually we get on the 10, curve briefly onto the PCH, and finally Ari pulls into the drop-off area at the start of the Santa Monica pier.

"You're really not coming?" I ask Ari as we get out.

"Hell no. Just supposed to drop you off. Dad says walk all the way out to the end."

Caleb and I get out. "Good luck," says Ari ominously, and with a squeal of tires he's gone.

11:51 a.m.

It's a brilliant day, cloudless and cooler here at the beach. Light curls of mist dance over the pounding surf. A bracing,

24

salty breeze rustles our hair and clothes. Caleb and I hold hands and make our way through the slow plod of tourists who are either meandering from one trinket shop to another, or lining up for the rides.

"Remember that thing Vic said?" I say to Caleb. "That Eli was staying at Jerrod's house for a while before Allegiance took off?"

He nods but is otherwise silent. Trapped in his own head. A prisoner once again, as other people change his world, over and over, completely out of his control.

We reach the end of the pier. Couples and families pose with the teal ocean behind them. I look around for Jerrod, barely knowing what he looks like.

A short set of warped wooden stairs leads down to a lower level, where fishermen cast their lines.

"There," says Caleb, pointing to one tall, bulky figure standing alone, leaning against the railing, smoking a cigarette.

We walk slowly down the steps.

"Mr. Fletcher?" I say, wondering why I'm speaking to him like a parent or teacher but some polite instinct kicking in anyway.

He glances at us, his face impassive. "Hi, Caleb. Hi, Summer." He turns back to the water. We join him leaning against the railing. For a second we just stand there, like tourists taking in the scenery.

Jerrod is in his fifties and looks the part of a successful

LA businessman: salt-and-pepper hair that's expertly windblown, still-youthful face but with deep lines around his eyes, short-sleeve button-down shirt with a pastel plaid print, khakis. The sandals are the big clue that he's not only successful, he's rich. There is no longer a need to impress anyone with footwear. They're probably still five-hundred-dollar sandals, but whatever.

I'm wound tight, but with each deep breath of the salty air, I also feel something free-falling inside that may actually be relief. Given our location, I understand that we have reached the end of at least one long lie. I grip Caleb's hand.

Jerrod takes a drag from his cigarette. Still not speaking.

Foamy swells plunk against the pylons below us. An older couple snipes in another language, maybe about fishing techniques, who knows.

"He left his wallet right here," Jerrod finally says, tapping the railing. "Along with an empty pint bottle of bourbon. There were about ten people scattered around who saw him climb up on the railing and dive out of sight."

Jerrod flicks his cigarette butt out into the water. "It was after dark, with a decent bank of fog. He was lost from sight pretty quick. A few eyewitnesses kept looking for him, waiting for him to surface, or call out for help . . . but he didn't. And just like that . . ." Jerrod snaps his fingers. "Eli White was gone."

I don't know what to say. Neither does Caleb.

Jerrod motions to the undulating water. "It's harder than you'd think to swim in those waves. Currents are tricky out there, too."

I look at all the blue. I've always been a fine swimmer but a tentative one. I have what I think is a pretty rational fear of drowning, and also of sharks and krakens.

"But not for a medal-winning swimmer," I say cautiously.

Jerrod nods. "A medal-winning JV swimmer, who quit after freshman year and never competed in a varsity meet. The early nineties were just primitive enough, internet-wise, that a fact like that never quite surfaced when Eli died. People like Charity and Randy knew, but for them it only enhanced the narrative: that Eli was strong enough a swimmer to try something stupid like this, especially while he was drunk and high, except this time he got in over his head. . . . So goes the cautionary tale."

"So you helped him," I say. "Fake his death."

Jerrod shrugs, which seems to be an admission. He stays silent, almost like he's not going to say any more . . . but then:

"It wasn't premeditated. Well, not really. If it had been, I'm sure we would have realized it was a crazy idea. The amount of work it's taken ever since, paying people to comb websites, to scrub away mentions of conspiracy theories or the lack of a body, most of all to manage the money. . . . But maybe we knew

27

that. Knew it was crazy, and that's why we didn't wait. . . ."

Jerrod takes off his sunglasses, squints in the reflection off the water, and puts them back on. "I was young. We both were. Not that much older than you. And I think we just thought everything would work out. I figured there was nothing in this world that couldn't be fixed. Maybe you feel that way sometimes."

"Not anymore," says Caleb.

"The point is, you look at the big choices you have to make, and you think you can see the two possible outcomes. But what you can't see are the outcomes beyond that. You have no idea how far the repercussions really go."

Jerrod pulls another cigarette from his pocket, along with a lighter, and lights up. "That's like, chaos theory, butterflies in China, or something?" He waves the cigarette at the water. "Anyway, we had no idea . . ."

He's being cryptic and it's annoying, but I feel like we need to let him go at his pace. After all, he's admitting to crimes here. I wish I'd thought to have my phone recording. A real gumshoe would be getting this on tape.

"Why did you do it?" Caleb asks.

"It was the money, mainly," says Jerrod. "You and your band mates are probably still doing all this for the art and the glory. But the first time you see your dream in dollars, it changes everything."

"We have some experience with that," I say, "thanks to you."

"Right. That offer probably threw you guys for a loop."

"Yeah," says Caleb.

"It's heartbreaking to watch bands erode," says Jerrod, "to see the bonds formed over a love of music get torn apart by bickering. You end up fighting about such stupid things: who gets the credit, who will potentially get the earnings on future success that may or may not ever happen. It killed me to watch Allegiance fall apart, to watch them eat each other alive. Eli most of all. But there was no way to stop it. Eli had his own problems that kept making the whole situation worse. He was looking for a way out. . . ."

"So . . . ," says Caleb, "you're saying that Eli really was thinking about suicide?"

"He couldn't see any other option," says Jerrod. "He thought death could be a reset button. Death also has a convenient way of defusing people's anger. Does the same for legal disputes."

"You said it wasn't premeditated," I point out, "but this sounds pretty well thought-out."

Jerrod shakes his head. "It was news to me, that night. I mean I should have guessed it. Eli suffered a lot. Depression, addiction, on top of all the band drama. He was always a deeply emotional person. The drugs and the missteps were a response to the way the noise of the world wore him down, rubbed him raw. . . . In a way, it was inevitable that he would try to silence it all."

"So you decided to help him."

"I decided to *save* him. But never before that night at my party." Jerrod makes a face that's either relieved or hurt. Maybe both. It's hard enough to tell what people my own age are thinking, never mind these cryptic adult faces.

"What exactly happened?" Caleb asks.

"I'm getting there," Jerrod says. At least he knows he's been beating around the bush. I wonder if we are the first people he's ever told this to.

"Eli and I were great friends," Jerrod continues. "After he ditched out on the band, he shacked up with Melanie in New York. I was the one who got him out of there. I sent him to London, to a rehab facility. He was there for a few weeks, that summer before he died. Got cleaned up for real. Meanwhile, the rest of Allegiance was lawyering up to sue him.

"When he came back to LA that September, he said he was seeing things clearly for the first time. He wanted to make peace with the band, settle the debts, and move on. But almost the second he landed, Kellen and the guys hit him with their lawsuit. They'd built a case to take him for way more than just the tour money he thought he owed them. They wanted all his future royalties on their music, and they wanted those last three songs he'd been holding back for *Into the Ever & After*. They said, and they were right, that until Eli turned over those three songs, he still belonged to Candy Shell. But there was no way Eli was giving them up. He denied they were even written, but we all knew better.

"So, that last night, he came to my house party, same night as Trial by Fire, as fate would have it. He made one last attempt at talking Kellen out of the lawsuit, but Kellen wouldn't listen. He wanted those last songs or there was no deal."

"But Eli had already hidden them, by then," I say, "for Caleb to find."

"Apparently. He never even admitted to *me* they were real, and I was his best friend, his only friend at that point."

"So you didn't know about these tapes?"

Jerrod shook his head. "Not until you started finding them. After you found the first one, I realized that Eli's old guitar case might be part of his plan. He'd asked me to give that to you, Caleb, when you were older, or if you ever came asking about him. To be honest I'd completely forgotten about it until Kellen and Jason explained to me what they thought you guys were up to. That's why I sent it along." Jerrod sighs. "It was so weird to see Eli on that tape you gave Kellen, sitting there in that bathroom . . . like seeing a ghost."

"Yeah," Caleb agreed quietly.

"I was at the Hollywood Bowl show, when he made that first tape. . . ." Jerrod loses himself in the waves for a second. "Anyway, that night at my party, things got heated. I didn't want there to be a brawl, so I pulled Eli up to my office. He was freaking out. In the biggest panic I'd ever seen. The lawsuit was going to bankrupt him, and it was going to take all the money he wanted to go to you." Jerrod pointed his cigarette at Caleb. "Then he tells me he's got a plan. The only thing he can think of. That he's been making preparations all week, and now he's got one last step. He's getting dark as he says this and suddenly I know where it's going.

"He holds up a fresh supply of heroin and a pint of bourbon. Says he's going to go down to the beach. Drink up, take a monster hit, and then swim away into the darkness. Once he's gone, he wanted me to talk Kellen and the guys out of the suit, to let it go out of pity, let his money go to you and your mom."

Caleb sighs quietly. I put my arm around him.

"He thought it was the only way out," says Jerrod, "the best way, for everyone. I told him he wasn't thinking clearly. We argued about it, but he wouldn't listen . . . and then suddenly the idea hit me. Maybe Eli was right. Maybe death was the right thing. Maybe it would work . . . if we set it up just right."

Jerrold takes a long drag from his cigarette. He's silent for a minute.

"So he was actually sober when he came down here," I say.

"He had his passport on him . . . ," says Jerrod. "I could see the fog on the water from my office. I called a guy I used for chartering yachts when we needed to show clients a good time. I knew he could be trusted: he'd seen rock stars and celebrities at their worst.

"And then I gave Eli a ziplock bag for his passport, and a couple hundred bucks in cash. I told him to act drunk and high on his way out. To make a scene. Even throw a punch at Kellen, which he was all too happy to do. Then drive to the pier, and make it look desperate. Car unlocked, spilled liquor on the seat . . . wallet and booze left behind. After he was gone, I took his stash of heroin and laid it out in the bathroom like he'd just used.

"And Eli played his part. He left my house in a perfect wasted, slurring, storming-out scene. Everybody saw it. Then he came right to this very spot and swam right out of his life. The boat was waiting offshore. I booked him on a red-eye to London. This was long before 9/11 and there weren't the same kind of records and scrutiny like now, not that anyone thought to look afterward."

"What about his body?" I ask.

Jerrod waves to the water. "He dove in with his clothes on, even his boots. Once he'd swam a little ways, he took them off—I had the captain bring a change of clothes—but it would be easy to believe that the clothes and boots would have kept him under. These currents stretch to Mexico. Lots of sharks out there. That part was easy. The trickier part was keeping that detail, the lack of a body, out of the coverage the followed, and the websites that would come along later. But there's people you can pay to keep track of such things, to erase details covertly, to conveniently delete pages. Probably wouldn't have been possible in today's world, but back then. . . . We nipped it in the bud. And at the end of the day, any conspiracy theory had to go against all of Eli's behavior leading up to that night. It's not like he was Kurt Cobain, with the suicide letter and those photos from the scene. He wasn't that famous anyway. And even back then, news cycles changed pretty quick.

"Once the world thought he was dead, I talked the band down. Instead of the lawsuit, Eli's assets and royalties went into accounts for you, and later your sister. Charity's been able to keep you in Mount Hope with that."

Caleb is lost in the waves, listening to this. All I can do is rub his back and press on. "So then what?"

"Then that's it," says Jerrod. "Eli promised to stay off the grid. He kept his word. He's been living under a fake name, I think. I was never in touch with him again directly until last week, when I arranged the meeting in New York. That was probably a mistake. Everything's at risk now. But . . . I knew how much you'd want to see him. That on some level, it wasn't fair that you never got to know him. I'm sorry it didn't work out."

"We want to try again," I say.

Jerrod shakes his head. "There's no way. It's too dangerous."

"I need to see him," says Caleb, finally reeling in his gaze. He stands up and faces Jerrod. "You tell him that."

34

"I can't. It was risky enough to get him the message about New York," says Jerrod. "And it wouldn't make a difference anyway. Eli hasn't answered any of my messages since Friday. It was a *huge* risk for him to come back. He had to use his real name on that ticket. His real address. I've got my people working overtime to make sure the wrong person never notices that, because if they do, all of this will have been for nothing."

"So what," says Caleb, "you're telling us *nice try, but sorry?*"

"I thought you should know the whole story," says Jerrod. "Now you do. But this is the price of knowing. If you tell anyone, you're sentencing him. I've advised him to go back underground for a while, and erase whatever tracks he's made. Maybe after some time has gone by, he'll feel like it's safe enough to contact you again."

"This is bullshit," says Caleb.

Jerrod sighs. "I wish things were different. I'll never be sure if we did the right thing. I hope you can forgive me, and him." He pushes back from the railing. "You'll have to take the bus back, I'm afraid. I can't be seen with you guys in my car."

"That's fine," I say, "we could use the time."

"I'm sorry I can't do more," says Jerrod . . .

And he walks away.

Caleb's gaze drifts out over the waves. "Wow."

"Hey," I say, hugging him. "It's okay."

"How can it possibly be okay?"

"Because we're going to find him. Whether he and Jerrod like it or not."

"But how?"

I wish I knew. "We have a thirty-minute bus ride to start figuring that out."

12:43 p.m.

"Where do we even start?" Caleb asks. We sit on the bus, crawling across the city. He leans against the window, his gaze empty, his face pale. He has dark circles under his eyes, as if each hour since I told him has been the equivalent of a sleepless night.

"I'm looking for shows we could get in London," I say. "There are a few indie festivals in the summer. . . ."

"That's so long from now."

"I know." I can't even imagine waiting until then. "There's got to be some way to get there sooner. We'll figure it out."

Caleb's fist lashes out, punching the back of the seat in front of us. An older woman glances back, scowling. "He's my fucking dad! And he's been alive my whole life. It was bad enough when everyone knew who he was while I didn't. But now. . ." He sighs. "Just once. He could have picked up

36

a phone *one time*, or sent an email, mysteriously appeared outside school in a hat and glasses, *anything*."

"It sounds like he and Jerrod were trying to protect you," I say carefully. "Or thought they were."

"For what?" Caleb can barely restrain his voice. "So I could have money? Who gives a—"

"Hey. I *know* . . ." I press a finger to his lips. Then my forehead to his. "It's so not fair to you. None of this is. He's a bastard for being alive just like he was a bastard for being dead. Either way, you're the one who lost out."

Caleb shakes his head. His voice cracks. "Why didn't he ever want to reach out?"

"Well, but he did, through the songs. And last week."

"Sixteen years later," says Caleb.

"But not never," I say. Caleb frowns at me. "I'm not trying to defend him. I'm just saying, that's why this matters now. Why we can't listen to Jerrod. Eli made the first move. Now it's our turn, no matter what he or Jerrod might want."

"But there's no way to find him," says Caleb. "Even if we went to London. It's kind of a big place. Jerrod was our only link."

We're silent for a while, heads leaning on one another.

I check my email and a new message makes me freeze up. "Look," I say, holding my phone so Caleb can see.

Dear Catherine,

I just wanted to say that it was a pleasure meeting you this weekend. The more I think about your journey, and your verve, the more impressed I become. I wanted you to know that I appreciate the effort you made, and I probably shouldn't be telling you this, but I have passed along an extremely favorable report to the admissions office.

Best of luck,
Andre

"You are totally getting in," Caleb says, and he manages to sound supportive, even though I know he wishes I wouldn't go. That instead I'd take next year off with him, get a job and save money and work on the band. Although who knows if that plan will make sense anymore after all this?

"I am possibly getting in," I say, and I feel like I might explode. It's like something has split open inside me, the uranium fuel cells melting down. Everything feels enormous and yet completely small.

I think of Dangerheart, all in the van somewhere in Utah, seeing the world and listening to music and feeling like the future was forever from now.

That was only a week ago.

I think of getting into Stanford and four years of college and graduation and jobs and apartments. It all feels like it is coming tomorrow. Like it's already done.

A few quick scenes and life is over.

So much is about to be decided.

Or maybe it's already *been* decided.

But I also remember being at UCLA back in December, visiting our family friend Stacia. The way the campus bubbled with ideas and enthusiasm in the twilight, students headed to wherever their passions might take them, and the sense that something profoundly freeing awaited me there, too: the chance to no longer be Summer or Catherine. The chance to balance both. And the chance to no longer be a "type" like we are in high school.

To be something in progress.

Who knows what I could become?

How can I feel that sense of possibility, but then also this sense of doom about the future already being decided, all at the same time?

It's making my insides boil and my outsides freeze. I just want life to be *now*. Not the future or the past. I want the moment I'm in to be everything for once.

I also remember the other thing I thought in the UCLA café. Maybe all of this is intense right now because this is the last six months I have here in Mount Hope, in high school, and at home.

Change is coming.

Maybe that change will be awesome.

But I can't even look at Caleb while I think that, and I don't even know how to deal with how sad that makes me.

He rubs his hand over the back of mine. "It's okay," he says quietly, sensing that now I'm the one with the overloaded brain. "We have time before you go. We don't need to think about that yet."

It's big of him to say. I wish I could believe him. Here I am *not* in the moment even though that's what I want.

Ugh.

"I know," I say. And I smile but it feels fake so I just lean my head into his shoulders and when the tears come I keep them as quiet as possible.

Caleb rubs my hair. He hears them anyway.

1:23 p.m.

We jostle over a brutal bump, and I snap awake. We're in a snarl of construction traffic. Both of us had dozed off, the heat and snail's pace of the bus lulling us into submission.

I start searching again for shows overseas. If not in London, how about France? There's a tunnel train; it's only a two-hour trip. Whatever we do, it has to be soon. Summer will be too late. Maybe there's something in the spring. April vacation is only six weeks away. . . .

Of course these searches assume we even have a band. We either need a new guitarist and bassist or we have to find Val and get Jon back. And can Matt even tour again after ending up in the ER last weekend? Did his parents find out about that? I mean, they must have, right? I planned on asking him today, before we ended up crossing the city.

"Anything?" Caleb asks.

"Not yet," I say. A festival in Madrid? That's not exactly England. . . .

Caleb's phone buzzes. "I might have something." He holds out his phone. "Check this out."

I take it and see a page of pictures. It's a Photobug account, and each photo is a thumbnail for an album. The page is titled *M. C. Fowler's Photos*.

"This is . . . Melanie's account? How did you get into this?"

Caleb makes a face somewhere between a smile and a grimace. "Val."

"You're in touch with her?"

"I have been since Saturday morning," says Caleb. "You were already on the flight back . . . and she swore me to secrecy. She said her mom's got the police looking for her."

"Is she at your house?"

41

"No, but she's in town. She took the bus all the way back to LA. Just got in this morning. Borrowed money from her friend Neeta, I guess. She's going to stay with a friend of one of her old band mates, in Manhattan Beach. She didn't even come back to our place for her car. I swear I was going to tell you soon. . . ."

"It's okay," I say. "I get it." I say this a little bit because I have to say it . . . but also I do understand. The fewer people know where Val is, the safer she is. And I know the jealous feeling I always have when it comes to Val is something I need to get over. I know she trusts me, too. But not as much as her brother.

"I texted her while we were in Ari's car," Caleb says. "About Eli being alive. When I told her about London, she sent the link to this account, and the password info. She said Melanie doesn't really use it anymore, and that a lot of the photos are from back when Val was a baby, and from before that. Back to when Eli was around. She thought there might be something here. She would have searched herself but she's trying to stay off her phone as much as possible. She's worried the police might be tracing it or something."

I scroll down, traveling back in time through Melanie's life. There's not much from these last ten years, but before that, the photos increase, including lots of shots of Val as a kid.

"Check this out," I say, tapping one album and enlarging a photo. It's Val at age four, naked except for a cowboy hat.

"She'd kill us if she knew we saw that," said Caleb.

42

"Yup," I say, clicking on it and saving it to my phone.

"Don't," says Caleb.

"Just this one," I say. "Sometime when this is all over, we'll show her and it will be hilarious."

I keep scrolling, past albums labeled *Christmas 1999, Rehoboth Beach* . . . And here's one . . .

"What's *Fowler Photography*?" I ask, clicking on it. The folder is dated 1999.

At the top are a few photos of the beach, of fog over the sand. The photos are arranged chronologically. I scroll down through a series of shots of the same street sign in different exposures.

Below that are black-and-white photos of Allegiance to North, very professional-looking. These are just like the photos that Melanie sent back at Christmas. There are live shots, the band members caught jumping around onstage, dripping sweat. And then a series of backstage candids. Their arms around guys and girls I don't know. Some are dressed like they're part of the industry, some look like fans. I check the dates on the photos: *June 1998*. One of the shows on the last tour . . .

"Melanie was good," says Caleb, looking over my shoulder.

I point to one near the end of the black-and-white set, showing Melanie between Eli and Kellen, an arm around each. "That's awkward."

"Yuck," says Caleb.

The next photos are Polaroids, scanned in. They are similar to the shots Melanie sent us. Washed-out images of her and Eli, of a rickety boardwalk and Eli with a soft-serve ice cream . . . maybe Coney Island?

Then I see a picture that stops my breath. "Here." It's Eli, standing outside a row of three-story brownstone apartments. He's wearing gold-framed sunglasses, a denim jacket, and torn black jeans. His arms are crossed over his chest, but he's holding up one hand, dangling a set of keys.

It's the same building we saw in the little painting in Eli's guitar case, and in the photo that we saw on the wall at Melanie Fowler's house. . . .This one is dated July 1998.

This is the place.

"There," says Caleb, pointing to the photo beside it. It's Eli in front of the same brownstone, but this time, in the corner of the frame we can see a street sign on the building wall. Only half visible, and blurry, but I can make out the letters "-ITH STREET." When I zoom in on the building behind Eli, I can read the number on the door: 55.

"On the 'Encore' tape, Eli called it the *summer Soho sessions*," I say. I hand Caleb his phone back and then open the map on my phone. Zoom out until I can scroll across the country, across the Atlantic. All the way to London. Soho neighborhood. I zoom in and slowly slide the map, scanning the street names.

"There," I say, holding up the phone. "Frith Street."

"Wow," says Caleb. He types a search for it into his

phone, then just stares at the little map. "I can't believe that's the spot. Like, where he is . . . wait." He zooms in. There's a little house-shaped icon floating over the address. He clicks on it. "Uh-oh."

The link takes him to a real estate page.

HOT NEW LISTING

55 Frith Street #3

AVAILABLE FOR RENT 3/1.

My heart starts to race. "That could just be a coincidence," I say.

"Jerrod told him to hide again," says Caleb. "He's going to run."

"March first . . . that's six days from now," I say. "But that might not be his apartment. He could be in another one. And just because he lived there a long time ago, doesn't mean he's still there . . ."

"Yeah, but these pictures with Melanie," says Caleb, "that little painting in the guitar case . . . This place was obviously important to him, sentimental. Jerrod said he's been using a fake name. Maybe once he got it all set up, it was safest to stay put?"

"But then he came to New York, and now Jerrod's telling him to disappear . . ." My brain is so overloaded that I start counting on my fingers. "He's been back from New York for two . . . maybe three days, depending on what time his flight was. It will take him at least a few days to move, won't it?"

"We can't get this close and then just lose him!" says Caleb.

Sitting there, I feel wild thoughts spinning in my head. Things a sensible person wouldn't say. But given everything we've been through, and now this picture, and even that email from Andre, I just say them anyway:

"What if we don't let him get away?"

"How are we going to stop him?"

"Let's go," I hear myself say, almost like someone has taken control of my body. Except I also feel like, *no*, this is me, really me, Summer and Catherine, all of us, my terrified, hopeful, brave core. "We have five days before the first of March. Five days to get to London before Eli moves. Eli will never expect us to show up right away. Neither will Jerrod."

"Because that would be crazy," says Caleb.

I can't help smiling, while also shivering inside. "Yes, it would be."

Caleb cracks a smile. But then it disappears. "But how the hell are we going to do that? There's no way to get a gig on that short notice, and besides there's school and the cost and no way our parents will go for it."

"But yours *will*," I say. "If you tell Charity and Randy about this? I bet they'd let you go. They might even come along. Either way, they'd help us. Don't you think?"

"Maybe," says Caleb. "But yours? That seems pretty unlikely."

I know he's right but I keep working through it, no matter how it makes my heart hammer. "They might if I'm going with you and your mom and Randy. And you know what? Why *shouldn't* they? They're getting everything they want from me. Their Stanford girl. And this is so important—"

"They just grounded you."

"They grounded me for being dishonest," I agree. "What if I'm finally honest?" These thoughts are rushing out of me, wild and half-formed but also things that have been bubbling in my brain ever since Dad bought me that plane ticket home from New York. The realization that I never truly express how I feel, that I predict what they think, label them Carlson Squared, and use that as an excuse to avoid telling them the truth about me.

The truths that would be difficult for them to hear.

But there again, I don't even know that for sure! It's not like I'm pregnant or taking drugs or want to join a cult or be a veterinarian. I just want to follow my passion for music. Not exactly scandalous. But it does go against the expectations that have been there my whole life.

The *plan*.

"I've never tried to really tell them how I actually feel about any of it," I say to Caleb, my words spilling out. "I always assume that I know what their answer will be. I've hidden some of my biggest dreams from them." As I say that, it feels impossible that I've let this happen. "What could it possibly hurt to ask them? And what could possibly be the big deal about missing, say, three days of school? I'm practically valedictorian."

"Yeah, but," Caleb says, "they're your parents."

"So what," I snap, "don't even try?"

Caleb grins. "God, no, that's not what I'm saying." He kisses me. "Yes, definitely try. It's completely crazy, but yes. We can have my mom call your parents, even. That will make them see how big a deal this is. They'd have to let you go, wouldn't they?"

I nod, my brain feeling spinny. "Maybe it would work. But what about Val?"

"Nothing's stopping her from coming except the same money issue we all have."

"And Matt? Do we see if he can go?"

"We at least tell him what we're up to and see what he thinks."

"And Jon?" I hate to even bring Jon up. He's a sore topic for all of us, but especially for Caleb. They disagreed the most, and I know Caleb feels on some level like Jon's departure was his fault.

Caleb stares out the window for a moment. "The whole drive home this weekend I was back and forth between *screw him* and *maybe we can get him back*. But . . . I don't trust him. He's so hooked in with Ethan and Jason now. I hate saying that. I just think it's too risky."

"Yeah," I say. I'm not ready to agree that we can't trust

him, but even just being reminded of the names Ethan and Jason makes my skin crawl.

"What about the cost?" says Caleb. "Should we ask my mom and Randy to pay for the plane tickets?"

"We can pay them back with show money," I say. "Summer jobs, anything we can do. My parents *should* be able to chip in, but let's ask Randy and Charity first."

I try to think of what we're missing. . . . "Passports. Do you have one?"

Caleb nods. "Mom and my grandmother took me to Italy when I was thirteen. You?"

"Mexico vacation," I say. "Do you think Val does?"

"I'll ask her." Caleb types into his phone.

I check the time. "We should be back by the end of school. If we talk to Matt, then go talk to your mom and Randy. . . . Then we try my parents tonight. Worst case, they say no and you go without me."

Caleb wraps his arm around me. "There's no way I'm going without you."

We kiss, and the warmth of it beats back the drumming of my nerves. "We could leave by Wednesday," I say hopefully. "We could be in London by the end of the week."

Caleb nods. "I'd say this is crazy, but, what hasn't been in all this?"

I kiss him again, and our faces stay together for a minute, breathing each other's air. "All we can do is try."

We walk past the main school doors just as the first students are rushing out. I already feel like a foreigner, like we've forever broken the bonds that keep us trapped in orbit around Mount Hope High day after day.

Everyone is chatting, laughing, rushing to the next thing. Part of me wishes my biggest worry today was band practice, or a PopArts project, or where Caleb and I were going on our next date. Classic senior year stuff. We pass my old friends, Jenna, Callie, and the rest, with a couple guys I don't know. I have this weird feeling, a sort of vague itch, like all of them bother me, or like I feel left out? Which doesn't really make sense. But I've given up on expecting all my feelings to make sense at this point. None of us make eye contact as I walk by.

Caleb and I head for the Green Room, staying outside school, buffeted by the exodus. I keep flipping back and forth between thinking we can pull off finding Eli and thinking it's insane. But if I've learned anything these past few months, it's that sometimes you just have to keep putting one foot in front of the other and not worrying about the what-ifs. There's a very good chance this won't work out, but until it's actually dead, there's still a chance.

The Green Room is already crowded when we arrive, but I see that the hierarchy of bands still applies, and that despite our current troubles, Dangerheart's table by the espresso bar remains vacant. Waiting for us.

As we cross the room, I hear a few whispers amidst the usual din: *Denver, New York, she ran away* . . . It's gossip but, in a way, the band might be even more revered, now that our road trip adventures have leaked out.

The question is, will any of the other members show up?

A few minutes later we get our answer: Matt, yes. Jon, no.

"Hey, Matty," I say, giving him a gentle hug before he sits down. His eye is still purple and swollen; so's his nose. Two butterfly bandages cross his eyebrow, a couple stitches beneath that. It's like an abstract artist has attacked his boyish features.

"Hi." He notices me noticing. His voice is muffled from the swelling.

"How are you feeling?" Caleb asks.

Matt smiles, but the injuries make it lopsided. "Not bad. The headaches have mostly gone away. Except for the headache that is my pissed-off parents."

"They weren't happy, huh?"

Matt laughs, but then winces, as if laughing hurts. "Randy called them from the ER, once we knew it was serious enough that I needed stitches and scans and stuff. So, they were prepared, and they even bought the story that I slipped on icy steps, but when they actually saw me last night? Yeah, they still freaked out."

"I'm sorry," I say.

Matt nods. "It's okay. So . . . ," he starts but then glances up and pauses.

Maya Barnes is at the front of the espresso line. She leans on the counter, eyes straight ahead, face stone.

"Hey, Maya," Matt says weakly.

Her face twitches, her eyes looking big and wet, but she shifts her body so she can't see us.

"Ouch," says Caleb quietly.

"That went well," says Matt with a sigh.

"I don't think either of us are very high on her list," I say.

Matt lowers his voice. "Any word from Val?"

"She's safe," says Caleb. "But I don't know many details."

"At least somebody's heard from her." Matt sounds like he wishes that was him.

"You're really into her, aren't you," I say.

Matt shrugs. "But I don't think it matters. We started hooking up months ago, but it always felt like it was just sort of random for her. Like she wasn't all there. I mean, I get it. . . ." It sounds like it still hurts.

I think of what Val said when we were going to her mom's house and I know that Matt's right. Not that Val isn't into him, but it's never going to be a crush or a real relationship, not now anyway. "She's going through a lot," I say, and it feels like a vague and lame thing to say, and it makes Matt's face fall because it sort of confirms what he suspected, but that's probably best for everyone.

"Has anybody talked to Jon?" he asks.

"No. You?"

"Nope."

"So, now what?" Matt wonders. "Find a guitarist? Practice for the release show?"

"Um . . ." I'd totally forgotten about our EP release show. I booked it right before we left on tour. It's a couple weeks from now at Haven, with All Hail Minions! "I should maybe reschedule that."

"Yeah. And what about Candy Shell?"

"Actually, things have gotten complicated. Listen . . . ," Caleb begins, and in a hushed voice he fills Matt in on what we know about Eli. "You can't tell anyone," he finishes, "under any circumstances. Swear it."

Matt is speechless for a second. "Sure, I swear. Let me guess: you want to go to London and find him before he disappears."

The way he says it cracks my fragile confidence. Like it's completely far-fetched. Even though I know he doesn't mean it that way, it gives voice to the very reasonable doubt I've been feeling, that there's no way we can pull this off. "That's what we're thinking," I say anyway. "Are you in?"

Matt's fingers run over the swollen skin beside his eye. "Come on, are you serious? There is no way I'm asking my parents for that. They would lose their minds. You guys go."

"We're a band," says Caleb.

"Sure," says Matt, "and we just got off an epic tour. But you're a family. Go figure it out, and we'll take it from there." Matt checks his watch. "I gotta get going. Mom's taking me for a second opinion on my face."

As Matt leaves, Caleb slumps in his seat.

"It's okay," I say, rubbing his leg. "We couldn't really expect him to come along, after what he's been through."

"I know. I just wish it could be all of us."

We grab much-needed americanos and get in Caleb's car. It's time to tell Charity and Randy, and hopefully get their help. We pull out of the parking lot and Caleb's phone buzzes. He checks it and hands it to me.

Val: Yes passport. Cruise with cousins, age fourteen. Drank rum. Not pretty.

"At least she's covered," I say. "Did you text your mom and Randy?"

"Yeah, I told them we wanted to chat after school, that it was important. No replies yet, though."

As we drive I check out airfare. "It's going to take a lot of gigs to pay back Randy and Charity, *if* they even go for this."

"How much?" Caleb asks.

"Like about fifteen hundred dollars each," I say, trying another travel site. "Looks like Wednesday would be the cheapest day to fly. Maybe if there's record label money . . ."

"The label," Caleb groans. "What are we going to tell Jason?"

"I don't know," I say. "One thing at a time."

"Okay. I— Oh shit."

"What?" I look up and see that we are turning onto Caleb's street.

And I see the police car parked in front of his house.

2:56 p.m.

Randy's stalker van is in the driveway. We park beside it and shuffle slowly up the walkway, holding hands, not speaking.

They are in the living room: Charity, Randy, a uniformed police officer, and another woman in a suit, sitting stiffly on the couches across from each other.

"Hi guys," says Charity, her face tight.

Caleb and I stand frozen in the doorway, no idea what to do.

"You're Caleb?" says the plainclothes officer, a badge around her neck. She checks a notepad. "And . . . Catherine?"

"Yes."

We both answer like it's elementary school attendance. My heart is slamming, and I can feel Caleb's hand shaking in mine.

"I'm Detective Reyes. We're here about Cassie Fowler. You two aren't in any trouble, but we do need to know everything you can tell us."

"It's okay," says Charity as we continue to stand there like statues. "They know you're related to her," she says to Caleb, "and I already told them that Val had been staying here up until last week."

"Ms. Fowler says she won't press charges as long as the girl is returned home," says the detective. "So if you cooperate, this should all go smoothly."

"If we can trust *Ms. Fowler*," Randy grumbles.

"Have a seat," says the officer, her face impassive.

Caleb and I shuffle to the kitchen table. Detective Reyes sits across from us. She leads with a smile. Trying to put us at ease. But it fades as she flips open her notebook, a pen poised over blank lines.

"So we know most everything," she begins. "Obviously you both care about Val, and you thought you were helping her by harboring her. Certainly having her in your home was safer than letting her sleep on the streets. Also, she's been part of your band."

"She's family," says Caleb.

"Of course. We understand the last time you saw her was in New York, is that correct?"

"Yes," says Caleb.

"And you haven't been in contact with her since."

"No," Caleb answers immediately.

Detective Reyes glances at Caleb, then jots down a note. There's something about these quick looks she gives us, like she can see right through any lie we might tell. I imagine her writing *liar*. "We'd like to get a few more details about the events in New York," she says, the searing glance aimed at me this time, and I feel my nerves explode. "Maybe we can start with your trip to the Fowler residence on February nineteenth."

Damn.

I don't want to look at Caleb. He stares hard into the table, but he might as well be glaring at me.

I never told him about my trip with Val to her old house.

Val didn't want me to. I'd meant to afterward, but there hasn't exactly been a chance. But now it looks like I've been holding out on him.

"We, um," I say, "Val wanted to get some things. She didn't want to go alone so I agreed. We kept it a secret because she knew it was risky."

Detective Reyes checks her notes. "Melanie says that Cassie stole money in the form of a blank check. Princeton police confirm that Val's fingerprints were on the checkbook and nightstand."

"It wasn't stealing," I say, although I guess it maybe was. "Val just wanted Melanie's account number so that she could send her money for her medical bills. Her boyfriend got the check back, anyway."

"We're not so concerned with that issue," says Detective Reyes. "The mother doesn't want to press charges for the breaking and entering or the theft, though technically she could. Our only concern is finding the girl and returning her to her home. We're just trying to get all the facts here. Did you take anything else from the Fowler residence?"

"Just a few personal things. Val grabbed her notebook, a shirt. I think that was it."

Detective Reyes's pen scribbles across the page.

I glance at Caleb. He's still staring into the table. "She didn't want me to tell you," I say to him. "But I was going to when we had the chance."

Caleb nods. "It's okay."

"I think that's all we need to know about that for the moment," says Reyes. "We have a pretty good idea of what happened outside the club last Friday night. Sounds like a disagreement between the boyfriend and your band member, Matt . . . And that's when Val ran off. Is that right?"

"Yeah," says Caleb.

"And you're sure you haven't had any contact with her since that night."

Time seems to stretch and the universe becomes untrustworthy. How fast should we respond? It feels like anything we do or say, even how we breathe or where we look or if our hands move will convey our guilt.

Caleb sighs. "Nothing since last Friday. I keep trying to text her, but . . ."

He sounds convincing, and Reyes nods. But now her eyes shift to me. I shake my head, feeling like every single movement I make screams guilt. "I haven't heard anything, either. I went back to the apartment where she was staying," I add, just to say something. "But she was already gone."

The officer speaks up. She's been still and expressionless this whole time. "If we checked your phones, or subpoena the phone records from your carriers, we wouldn't see any evidence of you communicating with her."

"You can't do that without a warrant," says Randy.

"Which we could get if it came to that," says Reyes sharply.

"No," says Caleb, stoic and believable.

"Nope," I add, hoping I'm half as convincing.

Detective Reyes traces over her notes with the back of her pen. I worry that she can see the truth, right there in everything we're not saying. . . .

She closes her notebook. "Those are all the questions we have at the moment." She glances at Charity. "You have our number. Because Ms. Fowler has filed a formal missing person's case, it is your legal obligation to let us know any information you might gain about Cassie's whereabouts."

"We understand," says Charity.

Detective Reyes stands. "I know that Cassie had her reasons for running away, and I know you want to help her. Once she is found, we've assigned a social worker to her case to monitor the home. But for the moment, from a legal standpoint, the best thing you can do is help us get her back to her mother. Remember that you're risking a civil suit if you don't cooperate."

Caleb and I nod quietly.

"Thanks," says Randy.

"We'll be in touch if there's anything else we need," says Detective Reyes.

After they leave, we all retreat to the living room, slumping to the couches.

"You've heard from her, haven't you?" says Randy, rubbing his hands over his face.

"She's okay," says Caleb. "Staying with a friend."

"Do you know where?" Charity asks.

"No."

Charity sighs. "I don't know if I want to know whether you're lying or not."

"Mom . . . ," Caleb starts.

"No, I mean it, Caleb," says Charity. "Believe me, I don't want Val going back to that woman, but . . . I feel like we can defend our decision to help her out, but the reality is that we harbored her for four months. If Melanie decided to come after us, she'd have a pretty good case."

"Except for the part where she's not a responsible parent and she hit her kid," says Caleb.

I think about the real story that Val told me: the fight she had with Melanie on Christmas Eve and how technically Val hit her first.

More secrets that only I know.

"But we can't really prove she's irresponsible," says Charity. "Can we?"

60

"Their house is a mess," I offer. "There's evidence of drug use everywhere."

"But they'd clean that up before any lawyers or police could find it," says Randy. "Maybe in time the social worker would figure it out. And ultimately, Val only has to make it another year until she's eighteen."

"But it's not fair," says Caleb. "We haven't just been harboring her, we've been *helping* her. Doesn't it matter that she's getting her GED and pursuing emancipation? She needs us if she's going to finish all that. Plus, it's not like she's really going to go home. If we turn her in, she's either going to run again or self-destruct."

"I know," says Charity.

"Can we talk to Melanie?" I wonder aloud. "What if you told her all this?"

Charity shakes her head. "I tried."

"You did?" says Caleb. "When?"

"Over the weekend. I called her after you told me Val had run again. Let's just say it didn't go well. I barely got past 'hello' before she started cursing me out. My call is probably what led her to go to the police. That woman . . ."

As we talk, I have this strange sensation, like there is a ghost at the table. A dark space missing from all of this . . .

It's Eli.

Missing not just from his son's life, but from his daughter's, too. His *family*. Except he's not a ghost. He's flesh and blood and hiding out in another world, and no matter what his legal issues would be, he's leaving his children without a parent. Val needs a dad. Especially with a mom like Melanie. She needs him around even more than Caleb does. Even just to have an opinion about what she should do. To be someone for her.

All of us are picking up the slack for Eli White.

And it's not fair.

The table has gotten quiet.

"You texted before," Randy finally says. "You wanted to talk to us about something?"

Caleb glances at me, and I try to tell him telepathically what I now realize we need to do. Luckily, he seems to be thinking the same thing. "It's nothing," he says. "We were going to ask you guys what you thought about the record label stuff . . . but it doesn't matter right now with all this going on."

"Are you still thinking Candy Shell?" Randy asks. "Didn't they want an answer today?"

"We were," I say. "And they do, but . . . we're not sure if we can do it without Val." That might not be the whole truth, but it is some small part of it. "We'll ask them for an extension."

I can feel the secret of Eli nearly bursting out of us, but we hold it in. We can't tell them, especially not now.

We have a short, hollow conversation about the record label options. The Candy Shell versus Jet City Records debate was the biggest thing in Dangerheart's world not much more than a week ago, but that now feels like something distant and barely visible.

Caleb says he's going to drive me home. We walk out, and I try to smile as I say good-bye, to fight the feeling that walls are closing in tighter all around us, that there's barely any room left to breathe.

3:42 p.m.

We are silent until we're in the car and around the corner.

"Did we do the right thing?" I wonder. "Not telling them about Eli?"

Caleb shrugs. "I wanted to, but . . . how can we right now?" He half whispers like there could be microphones anywhere. "We have to assume we're all being watched by the police. It's bad enough that my mom could get sued for harboring Val. If we tell her about Eli being alive, we're making her an accomplice to that, too, aren't we? Eli is a fugitive; he faked his own death and he's been hiding out in secret. And my mom is not one for breaking the law. With this Val stuff already going on, I don't think she'd last two seconds before she'd want to turn Eli in."

"She'd probably be right to want that," I say. "What if we only told Randy?"

"Maybe," says Caleb. "But the police will have their eye on him, too. And besides, wouldn't it be a crime for either of them to aid a runaway in flying out of the country . . . ? "

"That might be a crime for you and me, too."

"Maybe we should go, just the two of us."

I love that idea the second he says it. Just us, jetting off to London, like something out of a novel, and yet I can't believe I hear myself saying . . . "This is too important for Val, though." I tell him my thought back in his house, about Eli's ghost. "Eli should know how he's messing up everyone's lives with his absence. And Val needs him just as much as you do."

Caleb frowns. "You're right." He sounds so defeated. "So where exactly does that leave us?"

"I don't know . . . ," I say, "I think we have to ask my parents."

Caleb laughs. "You mean not only to let you go, but also to pay? Isn't that crazy?"

"Yes. It's completely crazy."

"What about your aunt Jeanine?"

I've already thought about her. She helped me pull off San Francisco . . . but this is different. "She's not going to go along with me leaving the country unless my parents are on board. That would be too big a lie."

"But your parents are still mad about the weekend."

"I know." *Believe me, I know.* "But they don't know about Val's runaway past. And Aunt Jeanine could help pay, if money was the only issue. I'm sure she would. So really, I just have to make them see how important this is." These thoughts feel shaky at best, but maybe, just maybe . . .

"What if I show them this email from Andre?" I say. "It would let them know that I'm still the girl they want me to be. I could even frame the trip as like, part of something I want to resolve before college."

"I know you don't mean it," says Caleb, "but it sounds like *I'm* something you need to resolve." He smiles, but it's for show.

"No, I don't mean that in a million years." And that feels like nearly the truth.

"But if you tell them Eli's alive, won't they want to tell the police?"

"Yeah, probably. Maybe I could just say that the trip is to find the third song. That's still pretty epic."

"Except they already grounded you over the trip to find the *second* song."

"I know," I say with a sigh. My nerves ring. This still all comes back to me being honest with them. About what's really at stake for me. I mean, they do love me. And they do know, I think, deep down, how important music is to me.

They *must* know that. Right?

And if they don't?

I guess it's time to find out. I don't know if I can make them listen. But I have to try.

We park in my driveway. Both my parents' cars are here. Mom works for a real estate company and business is slower in the winter. Dad gets up at like five every day because he's a nut about beating traffic. Also most of his business is with offices in other time zones. So they're both almost always home by the time I get home.

I just sit there in the car. The exhaustion from this day—or this week, maybe even this whole year—is really starting to set in. As is my doubt about whether my parents will listen to me. The idea of a grounded girl asking for a trip to London is about as insane as they come. But then again this whole situation is insane. Maybe it'll be like how two negatives equal a positive.

You know things are bad when you are looking to math for moral support.

"So . . . ," says Caleb. "Should I come in? Or . . . not."

"I think not," I say, not sure at all. "I have to convince them that this is what's right for me. If you're there they might dismiss it as me being irrational because I'm in love."

"Isn't that part of it?" I turn and see that Caleb is smiling, the most free he's seemed all day. His face lights up and it seems extra bright considering the clouds he's been under, and I have one of those crystalline moments where the rest of the world sort of shatters and falls away because you love this person, and he loves you back, and what else

66

really matters and DAMN this boy is hot. How do I even go five minutes without jumping him?

"Definitely," I say, rubbing my hand on his arm, letting my fingers mingle with his.

But Carlson Squared don't do irrational. I'm not sure when the last time was that they listened to their hearts.

Still, I keep sitting there.

My phone buzzes. When I check it, my gut tightens.

Jason: It's decision day. . . . And I haven't heard a peep.

I show Caleb, then put my phone on Do Not Disturb.

"We should probably just tell him no," says Caleb.

"Probably," I agree, but don't reply to the text.

"You sure you don't want me to come in?"

I lean over and kiss him, though my mouth is dry. My gut is flooded with adrenaline. "Nah. I'll text you with the verdict and we'll take it from there."

"Good luck," says Caleb. He doesn't mean to, but he sounds like he thinks I'm a goner.

So do I . . . but no. This has to work. Despite how much I want to run in the opposite direction, I can't keep avoiding them. I have to go in there and make them see.

I get out of the car. Caleb drives off. Step by step, I make my way into the house. I try to tell myself that this is no big deal. *Come on, Summer. You got this.* But I know it's a huge deal. I want to believe that what I'm about to ask for makes perfect sense, that I just have to make them see that. Except I worry that maybe it makes no sense.

My heart is racing. All this feels like some kind of reckoning.

Because to make them believe in what I'm asking for, I have to reveal a side of me that I've been hiding.

I have to be the real me.

First, though, I'll hit them with pride.

I take a deep breath and hold it as I walk through the door. "Guys, check it out," I say when I enter the kitchen. Dad is reading in the living room, sitting in his favorite stiff chair by the window. Mom is coming downstairs, probably because she saw me get home. Dad still in his work khakis and tie. Mom in a knee-length skirt and a cardigan sweater. All business.

Dad comes over and peers at my phone, adjusting his glasses. He looks sleepy; it's that time of day when he is fighting a nap the whole time. Naps are inefficient, after all.

"This is from Andre," he confirms, still reading. Then he straightens and looks at me with something like a smile, relieved, though still a little begrudging, given last weekend's events. I expect him to say something approving, but first he points Mom to the phone. "Take a look." As she's reading he looks at me. "What do you think?"

I don't know how to take the question. "It's . . . great," I say, and I think I feel like maybe I mean that. "Right?"

Mom finishes reading and she's beaming. "That is excellent, Cat." She gazes at me warmly. "All's well that ends well,

68

right?" She turns to the refrigerator. "Should we have some pie to celebrate?"

Her comment makes me squirm. It's like she's dismissing the past, brushing last week's little *incident* under the rug.

All's well that ends well.

So much of last week was amazing, not just a problem that needed a satisfactory ending . . .

Some of the biggest moments in my life . . .

"Actually," I say slowly, carefully, like tiptoeing through a minefield, "it's not really over."

Mom pulls the leftover pie from the fridge. She glances up at me, not saying anything, but it's as much of a *go on* as I guess I'll get. "What's up?" asks Dad. He's trying to sound casual, but at the same time he moves over to the bar and puts both hands on the counter, like he's bracing for whatever I might say.

"I have something to ask you guys," I say, "and I know it's going to sound like a crazy thing to ask, but it's also something that's super important to me, so before you say no, just . . . hear me out."

Carlson Squared share a glance.

"Okay," says Dad. He hasn't moved. Mom starts slicing pie.

The room is silent, the air still. Expectant.

Or lethal.

And I suddenly know that I should shut my mouth and

run. *Get out, Summer, before it's too late.*

But no. I won't. Not anymore.

"I know I messed up last week," I begin. "That you trusted me by letting me travel with the band, and that I betrayed that trust by lying to you about the interview. And maybe I don't deserve it, but this email makes it look like I'll probably get into Stanford. If not, there's still the other schools and I have those interviews in a couple weeks and all. My point is, I know you guys want me to go to college, and it looks like that's going to happen. . . ."

"Wait, I'm confused," says Dad. "Isn't that what you want, too?"

"Yes," I say, but ah crap there I am immediately lying. It's like I duck before I even think! Except, there *have* been moments when I've wanted to go. Not nearly as many as the moments where I've known I'm *supposed to* want to, but still. *Keep talking . . .*

"But I've actually been struggling this fall because while part of me does want to go to college next year, another part of me wants to . . ."

Say it, Summer.

I can't.

Oh, God, be the girl you want to be and say it!

Deep breath . . .

"Part of me doesn't."

Mom places the first slice on a plate.

"What do you mean?" Dad asks.

"Well," I say, "it's just that, another part of me imagines something different. I love music so much . . . I don't know if you guys even know that."

"Cat," says Dad, "we know that."

Do you, really, though? "Well, maybe, but I don't think I've really told you *how* much. Like I love working with bands, like with Dangerheart, and part of me sometimes thinks about . . ." *Don't say it! You have to. This is now or never* . . . I feel myself seizing up as the words come out: ". . . taking next year to work on the band full-time, to get further in the music scene, like maybe an internship, and really go for it like I can't do while I'm in high school, or . . . from college."

"You mean like, not even going to college next year?" Dad asks. He's still staring at the counter, both hands planted. Mom is putting the pie away.

"Maybe, yeah," I say. "I mean I definitely want to go to college, at some point, I think. But music . . . it's what I dream about, what I've imagined, I—I don't know."

"Is that what you want to ask us?" Dad says slowly. "To take a year off before college?"

"No, I mean, not yet. It's something I've thought about but I'm not sure yet. I'm still trying to figure it out. I just wanted you to know that it was . . . a thing. On my mind."

Another deep breath. Hands clasped because they're shaking. "What I really wanted to ask you is about Dangerheart. We know . . ." I pause again, my nerve failing . . . *almost there*. Just have to get this out. "Remember I told you about Eli White's lost tapes . . . we know where the third one is, now. It's actually in London and . . . we want to go get it."

Silence. It occurs to me that I barely spent two minutes trying to tell the truth and I'm already back to lying. Oh well. There's no going back now.

So I stumble on: "It—it's important to Caleb and Val, but it would also be huge for the band. I mean, we've come this far, and to find all those lost songs would be amazing. And then this whole big search would be over. No more asking to go on crazy trips or anything. And we can make the money back from gigs, and it would only be a few days of school and then, like I said, this would be behind us and—"

There's a flat smack as Mom places a trio of forks on the counter. "Wait," she says. "You're asking to go to London."

"Yes, just to find this last tape."

"Not a week after you lied your way to New York. . . ."

"I didn't—" but I stop. Even though that's not exactly how it happened, or maybe it kind of is, I need to focus on the goal here. "Yes, I guess that's true."

"When are you proposing to do this?" Dad asks.

"Well, it would be best to do it soon, so that we have the song and we can—"

"How soon?"

It seems totally insane to say this. "This week."

Mom looks at Dad. Dad looks at Mom.

And of course I know. Obviously the answer will be no.

I can barely believe I'm letting these words come out of my mouth. There is no possible way that they are going to go for this. And each silent second feels like a year.

"Cat," Dad finally says. His eyes flash to mine but then his gaze settles somewhere back on the counter. "Where is all this coming from? I mean, you're running off with this band, missing school—"

"It would just be a couple days," I repeat.

"It's not just that," Mom says, and suddenly her tone has gone cold. "The office called today. We know you skipped all of your classes after third period."

"Oh, that . . ." Crap! Busted again. "Well, it was because Caleb and I had to talk about this lost song. We'd just figured out where it was, which is why I'm here now. If we went and found it then we wouldn't have to miss any more school or anything I swear—"

"Okay, enough," says Dad. He doesn't sound mad . . . but getting there. "Caleb seemed like a nice enough kid the few times we've met him, but this is all getting out of hand. Cat, I know you're in love, and this lost song business is certainly intriguing, but you can't just fly off to London and miss school, and you can't just talk about taking a year off to mess around with your band."

"Dad, it's not messing around!" I know I sound petulant when I say this, but I can't help it with my heart on overdrive.

"But you're going to have so many years after college,"

Mom says. "If you get out of school and you want to manage bands, you'll have a whole decade in your twenties. I know that seems like forever from now, but it's not. Take it from us. You're going to have so much time for things like this: band shows, impromptu trips to Europe. Or who knows, maybe even as a graduation present. Cat . . . I think you just . . . you have to see the bigger picture here."

I can hear the *no* between every word and it's tearing me apart. "Mom, my twenties are forever from now! And besides, this *is* the bigger picture. This is a once-in-a-lifetime chance to do something amazing, and it's right there for the taking. Let me go to London and I'll go to Stanford like a good girl—" Where are these words coming from? Desperate. Am I even serious? Or just spinning more lies— "And I won't even fuss about it."

"See? *That* kind of talk, right there," says Dad, his voice rising. "It's not being a *good little girl* to go to college. It seems like ever since you started dating this boy, you— This just isn't the Cat we know."

"That's my point!" I say. "Maybe I'm not the little *Cat* you think you know. But that doesn't have anything to do with Caleb. It's what I'm trying to tell you—"

But Dad isn't hearing me. "How can you expect us to believe you after last week? How can we trust you? If we let you do this, you're just more likely to . . ." He throws up his hands. "You'll want to go on tour all summer, miss college, or worse, start college and drop out and ruin your future chances. Where is it going to end?"

"Dad, that's not how it's going to be!"

But Dad shakes his head like he's made up his mind. "I think you're in over your head here, Cat. This world of music and musicians is clearly messing with your thinking in some unhelpful ways. I mean, we are talking about tapes left by a drug addict who killed himself and abandoned his family! He is no hero."

It takes all my will not to respond. I bite my lip hard as the tears come.

"I know you love working with this band," says Dad, "but . . . you're not even *in* the band."

"Wow," I mutter.

"That's not—" says Dad. "What I mean is you're a girl on a *trajectory*, a high achiever, college-bound, and I'm sorry but we're just not going to let this band preoccupation derail your potential. It has to stop."

"Dad, it's not a *preoccupation*," I say, my voice tight, trying not to sob. "It's a passion!"

"Then maybe you need to find another passion!" Dad balls his fist and I see him shake off a surge of anger. "I'm sorry, Cat, but, man! You have academics. You had volleyball . . . We've stood by and let you shun so many other possibilities in school, things like student government . . . Honestly you're lucky, damn lucky, to still be getting considered for a school like Stanford with all the time you waste on these bands! It is a privilege to have what you have, and to listen to you take

75

it for granted, and to ask for these silly things is . . . I've had enough! Taking that phone call from Andre, having to fly you home, watching you slouch around that scummy practice space . . . it's not you, Catherine! It's not you."

I'm crying now. Full-on.

But I'm not going to yell anymore.

The cards are finally on the table.

"It is me," I say quietly.

My tears have the predictable effect of bringing Dad down a notch. I sort of hate that, the power of my weakness. No cheat codes. But I can't help crying.

"Look, I'm sorry to get so angry . . ." But he doesn't finish.

Mom sighs. "I agree with your father. I know it may be hard to understand where we're coming from—"

"No," I say, still crying, but firm. "No, I get it. I totally get it."

We stand there silent. Mom rearranges the pie plates, but doesn't ask us if we want any. There will be no family snack time now.

"You have so much potential," Dad says. "I just . . ." He looks so disappointed, so sad, like he might cry, too. And, God, on top of *all* of this, the guilt that I am letting him down nearly pushes me under completely. "I just don't understand why you're not content."

If it were possible I would laugh. I think of my college essay, the one I wrote at Canter's at four in the morning, still easily the weirdest, or maybe truest, thing that's ever come out of my head.

Maybe the only thing I'm content in is my discontent.

Oh hell, Summer.

"I'm going upstairs," I say, wiping my nose. "Thanks for listening." I shouldn't have added that last comment, but I couldn't help it.

"Let's talk more later," says Mom, in damage-control mode.

"Right."

4:31 p.m.

I have my phone out by the time I'm at the top of the stairs.

I send the first text when I'm in my room, door shut. When I get the answer I want, I breathe deep, hearing only the deafening hammering in my chest, thudding inside my ears.

I check a couple websites. Do some quick math on the calculator.

Text again.

And wait.

The answer arrives. Again, unlike downstairs, Summer gets what she wants.

And so finally I text Caleb.

Summer: Are you home yet?

Caleb: What if I told you I was parked around the corner from your house.

Summer: I would say that I love you and you are the bestest.

Caleb: Should I come get you?

Summer: No, I'll come to you. Sit tight. I'll say I'm taking the bus to meet Maya or something. Doesn't matter. They'll know I need some time to cool off.

Caleb: That bad, huh?

Summer: Worse.

My fingers tremble, the nerves buzzing, my skin electric.

Summer: Caleb?

Caleb: Yeah?

Summer: What if we went tonight?

4:56 p.m.

Our first stop is the Hive. We pass through the usual gateway cloud of cigarette and weed smoke, sidestep the empty bottles spilled over from the trash cans by the door, the legs of musicians sitting in the hall. It's all I can do not to wave away the smoke, trying to keep my fresh outfit of clothes clean for as long as possible.

They'll need to last awhile.

On the way over, I checked my shoulder bag at least ten times. Phone. Phone charger. Passport. Driver's license. Extra underwear. One pair of socks. A spare T-shirt. Toothbrush and some makeup. All the cash I had: a stunning thirty-two dollars. I changed into clean jeans, a long underwear top under a T-shirt, and a hoodie. Everything a good girl needs for a three-day international trip when she also has to walk out of the house looking like she's just going to the mall for an hour.

This is insane. I know it. The day has spiraled so far from where it began. And at this point, it feels like to stop moving would cause everything to collapse around us.

We hurry up to the practice space. Caleb is pulling the key from his pocket when we both pause, our eyes meeting.

There's music coming from inside. A song I know too well.

"Shit," Caleb mutters. He opens the door.

Jon is kneeling by his amp, wrapping up cables and putting them in a black duffel bag. His phone is plugged into the PA and blaring a song by Postcards from Ariel. My old band, his new band. Hearing Ethan's voice makes me tighten up, and I hate that he still has that effect on me.

Jon looks up. Sees us. Looks away fast.

"Boning up on your new band?" Caleb asks. He's trying to look indifferent, standing there with his arms folded, but he can't hide the hurt in his voice. I rub his arm, hoping we can avoid a fight. We have way bigger problems than Jon right now.

And apparently Jon has bigger concerns than us.

"Got a show tonight," he says. He reaches over and taps his phone, silencing the song, and returns to packing away cables and pedals.

He unplugs his amp, tucks the cord in the back. He's already taken down the Christmas lights he hung on the ceiling. There's a blank spot on the wall where his vintage Rush *2112* poster used to hang.

And it hits me that it's really over. We're not going to lose Jon.

We've already lost him.

I'm on the verge of tears again. "You're moving out for good," I say.

Jon sighs. He doesn't look up. I wonder if maybe he can't. "They practice over at the Cubes, so . . ." He zips up his bag and stands.

Caleb still hasn't moved. We are between Jon and the door. Which means he finally has to look at us.

"I'm sorry," says Jon. One part of me wonders if he needs to be sorry for anything. He hated being over-shadowed. He *did* get overshadowed. This band has been anything but normal. Still . . . we could have made it work. I want to launch into it with Jon all over again, about how we just have to get through this business of Eli White, and then things will be normal, except how true could that possibly be, especially if we find him alive?

"It's cool," says Caleb, which is musician speak for *whatever*. He's done.

"Jon . . . ," I start, because this feels wrong. No matter what went down last week, we were good, Dangerheart was *great* with Jon, and sure, there are a million guitarists, a hundred right here in the Hive, but they are the unknown.

Jon was ours.

And he was with us at the beginning. It's never the same after a band's original lineup. The ones who first took the stage together. There's a bond there, some love that comes from starting it, from working your way up together. Anyone who comes after . . . it's all a little bit less like family, and just a bit more like business.

Jon looks at me, waiting for me to add something.

I want to tell him that I'll call him next week, that we'll talk it out, but even saying a phrase like "next week" opens the slightest window into what we're doing *this* week, and that's a secret—there have been so many secrets—that we just can't trust him with anymore.

So instead, all I say is: "Break a leg."

Jon nods, eyes back to the floor. "Thanks." He shuffles past us, lugging his amp, guitar over his shoulder. "See you guys around."

We should hug or something . . .

Say something more. Anything.

Hey Jon, remember that time driving to San Francisco? Singing Allegiance to North songs, you playing guitar in the back? When everything was new and we were free?

Remember . . .

But he's out the door and gone.

I start crying but I don't want to be. There's been enough of that. I hold my breath, keep silent. Dammit.

"Postcards is a great fit for him," says Caleb.

"It . . ." I can't disagree.

Caleb sighs. "Come on, we need to keep moving."

I nod, close the door, and work on the simple act of breathing and making it through each second, as Caleb digs into the recesses behind the sagging couch, gathering the hidden items that we need for what comes next.

6:07 p.m.

I slap the videotapes on the table.

"There you go," I say. I draw my hand back and rest my fingers on the linoleum inches away. As soon I lose touch with them I immediately want to snatch them back, to tuck those little plastic cases safely back in my bag.

But it's too late for that now.

There they sit, "Exile" and "Encore to an Empty Room," the lost songs of Eli White. Videos from the great beyond, now back home on a chipped linoleum table, beneath an evening autumn sky, their sky, perhaps the very ceiling that inspired their creator in the first place, sitting here at Canter's the night after a gig, so many years ago.

For a second, Jason Fletcher doesn't say anything. His hungry shark's grin lessens, and he looks almost . . . shocked.

"Anybody need a refill?"

The narrow shadow of Vic appears beside us, holding

82

the stained coffeepot. I watch him as he notices the tapes on the table. His expression doesn't change, but he glances at me. I offer him a weak smile that I hope somehow says, *Yeah, I know, but this is what we had to do.*

Vic has zero response. "No?" he says.

"I'm good," says Jason, not bothering to make eye contact.

"I think we're set," I say. "Thanks, Vic."

He flashes a disapproving glance at Jason. Then looks back to me. "You let me know, anything you need."

He stalks off.

Jason is still gazing at the tapes.

"I was just old enough when Allegiance was really hitting it big," he says. "My dad gave me *The Breaks* for my tenth birthday. They were my first favorite band." I never thought it was possible that Jason could be so . . . reverent about anything, and though my opinion of him isn't changing, it does remind me that it's unfair to think that anyone is purely one-dimensional.

"I used to sit around reading every rumor about *Into the Ever & After*. I'd overheard my dad's conversations, so I knew the band was going sideways. I was even there backstage for a couple of the big fights between Eli and Kellen. But like a naive kid, I thought if they could just get that second album out they would be okay. Shit . . ." He shakes his head. "I had a poster of Eli White on my *wall*."

A little voice in my head reminds me to check my watch,

and seeing the time breaks the spell of this weird human moment with our otherwise-nemesis.

"Are you going to take them?" I ask. As I do, I reach over and rub Caleb's knee. He's staring at the tapes, too.

"It's just," Caleb had said in the car on the way over here, "the tapes are my only lifeline to him. If we *don't* find him . . ."

But I know he agrees that this is our only move.

"Hell yes, I'm going to take them." Jason lays his hand over the cases and slides the tapes close to him. Once they are in his clutches, he checks each box to make sure there's actually a tape inside. "I know this is what *I* would do, if I was in your position," Jason says. "But . . . since it's you guys, I can't help but wonder if there's a catch. . . ."

"You offered us a deal," I say quickly, trying to sound professional. "We're taking the deal."

"So it appears." Jason glances over his shoulder and snaps his fingers. Side note: finger snapping? What an ass.

Maya Barnes appears. She's actually been standing over by the counter at the entrance to the restaurant this whole time, hate-watching our little meeting. I can't decide whether I feel bad for her being treated as the lowly intern, or satisfied after how she sold us out in New York. Of course, she had her cheating-boyfriend reasons for revenge. So mostly I'm just trying to avoid the laser-death glare she's been giving me since we arrived.

Jason holds the tapes up to Maya. "Check them."

Maya nods, her face red, tight. She's wearing all black. Her hair is up but a long strand has sprung loose, trailing down over her thick-rimmed glasses. She keeps brushing it behind her ear, but it keeps falling back down. Now that she's this close there's no way she's looking at me.

She digs into her big black shoulder bag and produces a vintage camcorder. She pops in the first tape, fast-forwards a little, then holds it out so Jason can see the screen.

The tapes hisses. We hear Eli's tinny voice: "*Hey, far comet . . .*"

"Excellent," says Jason.

Maya pops out the tape and they check the other. Same result. She hands the tapes back to Jason. "Thanks, Maya," he says, waving her away.

"Sure," Maya mumbles. She marches off, no doubt so, so furious. It breaks my heart a little, but mostly I'm just relieved that she's gone. My nerves feel like tightropes, humming in the wind, and they can only balance so many things at once.

Jason sighs dramatically. "Well, then. Here we are, at last. I have my Dangerheart, and Eli White has returned to his final resting place. I have to say, I *never* thought you'd give these up."

Caleb and I say nothing. He squeezes my hand because I know he's regretting it, even if it will get us what we want.

"That said . . ." Jason gives us the side eye. "You know I need to ask you about the third tape."

I shrug. Luckily for once, I can pretty much just tell the truth. "We thought it was going to be in New York. You were there when we checked the Hard Rock, and Ten Below Zero. That was where all the clues led, but . . . it was a dead end."

Ha-ha, more like the opposite!

Oh, if only *anything* were funny right now.

"We've learned that my dad wasn't exactly the master planner," Caleb adds. It's the perfect line.

Jason nods and his smile fades. "I think Eli ended up letting a lot of people down."

Jason has always been good at hiding what he really thinks. Still, I'm pretty sure he buys our story. He was there in New York. He had his eyes on us. He had no idea that was actually Eli onstage at Ten Below Zero, and he'd never heard "Encore to an Empty Room" to even realize that's what was being played as he walked in.

And, like everyone else, his default belief about Eli White is forever cemented by his dad's trickery: Eli the tragic figure, who took himself down. Who let down his fans. And Jason was one of those fans.

"Still," says Jason, upbeat, "even just two tapes hidden across the country makes for an amazing story."

"What are you going to do with them?" Caleb asks.

"I've already got a deal lined up for a documentary. Kellen and the boys will record the songs. And we're going to reissue *Into the Ever & After*. Not quite complete . . . but close enough." He looks at Caleb. "Now that you're a Candy Shell artist, we would love to prominently include you and Dangerheart. The story of Eli's son finding the tapes, tracking them down across the country. That will be *huge*."

Don't we know it. We imagined that so many times, only we hoped it would be on our terms, not Jason's.

Caleb just nods but doesn't respond.

"You can think about it," says Jason. "Take your time."

My phone buzzes. My heart skips when I see the text.

Dad: We're saving you a plate of dinner. Lasagna. We expect you home soon.

I feel like I might cough my heart right out onto the table. I click off the screen. "So," I say, trying to focus, "you have the tapes. We did what you wanted. . . ."

"You did . . . ," says Jason, and his grin returns. Suddenly I wonder if we've been duped. This was our only shot. . . .

"And think what you want of me," he says, "but when I make a deal, I stick to it."

Jason reaches into his jacket pocket and pulls out a long envelope. He lays it on the table, but keeps his hand on top of it. "I have to say, I am sort of wondering why you need this." He taps the envelope, and his voice dips back into that oil-slicked tone we know so well. "And where are the rest of your band mates? Shouldn't this be a group decision? Unless you've both decided to screw them over and take it all for yourself. . . ."

I hold my breath, knowing I have to both keep my cool and lie more, but also because in order for the lie to work, we have to be honest about a few things. Hello, tightropes!

"Matt is recovering from the injuries he got in New York," I say. I can't help narrowing my eyes for what I say next: "Don't act like you don't know where Jon is."

Jason grins sheepishly, just like a wolf. "Well, yeah, I guess you'll be needing a new guitarist. I know a few guys."

"We'll find one," says Caleb. "On our own."

"Suit yourself," says Jason. "I'm here to help. And what about your little runaway?"

"Val's mom has the police searching for her," I say. "But she's going to pursue emancipation." I glance at the envelope. "That's the biggest reason why we need this. She can't wait however many weeks it would take to sign the contract with you guys and all that."

"It does take forever," says Jason. He taps the envelope. Eyes us. Taps it again . . .

And slides it over.

"Congratulations, Dangerheart. You are officially signed to Candy Shell Records. Ms. Barnes over there is our witness to this exchange, a supplemental advance on your advance."

I place my hand over the thick envelope. "And your boss dad is okay with this?" I ask nervously.

"I don't have to check with Daddy before every move

I make," Jason says with just the note of stubborn defiance that I hoped to hear. "It's my job to bring in the talent. He trusts me to do that in whatever way *I* see fit. This little sum is well worth the reward."

Perfect, I think. *Keep your dad out of this, Jason, for just a little longer. . . .*

Jason glances back at Maya then lowers his voice a touch. "Still, whatever you need to do about your Val, when it comes to the police and all that, I want to know nothing."

I slide the envelope over to us, feel the stack of bills inside, but don't open it, even though my fingers are twitching to do so.

"So, should we get some food to celebrate?" Jason asks. "It's on me. After all, it's a business expense now."

"No thanks," I say. "We're going to celebrate on our own."

Jason nods. "I so barely trust you guys right now," he says, and then taps the tapes against the table. "But I also barely care. Even if you were to jet off right after this meal and go find the third tape, you took our money, so . . ."

"What?" says Caleb. "You own us?"

Jason laughs. "Of course not." Then his tone lowers. "Just your music."

A cold wave ripples through me. I take Caleb's hand under the table. It's clammy. Oh man, what did we just do?

Jason stands. "Can't wait to work with you guys." He sticks out his hand.

Though it's the last thing we want to do, we shake.

Sometimes you have to make a deal with the devil.

7:16 p.m.

It turns out, even in this era of security and credit cards and mileage accounts, you can still walk into an airport and buy a plane ticket. Or, three tickets. You can show your passports, and then thumb hundred-dollar bills out of an unmarked white envelope, one thousand five hundred dollars, times three. You can even get some change back.

It turns out the ticket agent won't even blink.

It also turns out you can walk nearly the entire way from long-term parking to the ticket counters at LAX without breathing.

Do I ever breathe anymore?

I'm getting oxygen somehow, and energy, but God knows from where. I haven't eaten a thing since breakfast.

When I was eating breakfast, Caleb didn't even know yet that his father was alive. A little over twelve hours ago. Tepidly pushing instant oatmeal around in a bowl, taking meager bites while deciding if I would even tell Caleb at all.

Eight hours later, here we are and everything has changed but when Caleb asks if I want anything from Au Bon Pain after the tickets are bought, my stomach growls a firm "hell no."

Val was waiting for us inside the terminal, sitting sideways in a row of black airport chairs, knees to her chest, flipping her finger over her phone, small backpack by her side. When we first saw her through the blur of bodies in transit, a ghost world of identities between destinations, I almost cried. Little Val, lost sister, not to me, but still. Caleb broke into a jog, and the two of them hugged like family. I slowed my pace to get there a moment later.

She hugged Caleb hard. Of course all she and I said to each other was, "Hey." But it's a *hey* that has history now. Miles in the van, fights, secret trips to old homes, and more miles to go. I feel closer to her than most of the people I've known a hundred times as long. I don't know where she's been these last few days; I'm just glad she's here.

"So," she said, "let's do something crazy." She slung her bag over her slight, wiry frame, brushed her newly lavender hair from her eyes, and we headed for the ticket counter.

It turns out, Val's passport identifies hers as Cassidy Elizabeth Fowler, and mine identifies me as Catherine Summer Carlson.

And Caleb's middle name is Richard?

"No dick jokes," says Caleb.

And so for the five minutes that we talk to the ticket agent, we are the children our parents named us, the models they created, only now our programming has evolved and grown sentient.

We have gone rogue, and if any of them knew where we were now . . .

If any of them knew.

7:38 p.m.

The security line is the last moment. We step to the man at his little podium and he runs our passports under his little blue light. Checks our tickets.

I am so sure that we will be pulled aside, that officers will converge from unseen locations, that our parents are waiting for us somewhere nearby.

But he just waves us on.

They scan us, and though we are the bones and blood and dreams of our parents, we are also our own unique selves, and it turns out, we are allowed to dream and plot and defy and break, break, break the very rules of our universe.

"We are flying to *London* . . . ," Val whispers as we walk together, the three of us, post-security.

People dart around us, on their way to everywhere.

"Is this really going to work?" she asks.

"I think so," says Caleb, his breath tight, too.

We stop and check the Departures screen to be sure of our gate. We are flying Icelandair, because the only nonstop flights leaving tonight were sold out. Even that is some kind of amazing. On a random Monday in February, there are that many people who are traveling to another continent, and London is only one city on one continent, one name in the *L*'s on the huge departure board of possibility.

There are so many possibilities . . .

It feels like we can be anything.

We are only tied down by our expectations and desires.

Well, and let's be honest, by our lack of fat envelopes of cash from slimy record labels.

But still.

Here we go.

And it is something like all of the universe right there between your heart and your ribs.

Holy shit.

Yes!

Despite all of the risk in what we're doing, I am suddenly gripped by some kind of elation. Sheer terror? Perhaps. But it's making me smile and I push against Caleb. He tugs me out of the fray of moving people. We stumble to the wall and crush against each other and make out.

"Ugh," says Val from up ahead.

"Sorry," Caleb says as he takes me by the hand and we catch up.

"I'm so glad we're not sitting together," says Val. Her seat is a few rows behind ours.

We all smile.

And manage to eat burritos.

And make it to the gate.

8:50 p.m.

"Welcome aboard, Ms. Carlson," the gate attendant says to me.

And we walk down the Jetway to our spacecraft.
It turns out, we are flying to London!
But hold on . . .
There is one more thing to do.

9:08 p.m.

"Ladies and gentlemen, in just a moment we'll be closing the forward door. Please take this opportunity to make sure all your devices are in airplane mode."

Caleb: Mom, I'm so sorry. Because of the police, I can only tell you this now. I'm on my way to London. It's about Dad . . .
Caleb: Don't worry. We bought a round-trip ticket and will be back on Friday. Please trust me. We have to see this through. I love you and I'll keep you updated. -C

Summer: . . .

"Ladies and gentlemen, the forward door is now closed. Flight attendants will be coming through the cabin to make sure that all your carry-on items are stowed and electronics are in airplane mode."

Summer: Mom. Dad. I am so sorry. I'm sorry to disobey you

I delete all that.

"Miss?" The flight attendant looks around Caleb to where I'm slouched over my phone.

"Sorry," I say, "doing it now."

Shit.

My thumbs tremble over the keypad. I don't know what to say. I have to at least tell them the facts:

Summer: Dear Mom and Dad: I'm on Icelandair Flight 2043 to London. I am with Caleb and Val and we will be back on Friday. I have money and my passport and we will be safe. I

"Ma'am . . ." Another flight attendant.

I stare at the screen.

Summer: I don't know exactly what I can be, but I know I can't be exactly what you want. I need this trip. I need this week. I'm really, really sorry and I love you.

"That's good," Caleb says over my shoulder. "That's enough."

Still not breathing.

I hit send.

There is a light bump as the plane lurches back from the gate. Suddenly tears are streaming down my face.

Caleb rubs my back. "We'll be okay."

I grip his hand. "I know."

And I do. I really do.

I watch out the window as the worker waves his double red lights, guiding us out onto the tarmac, the launch pad, out of our orbit and our lives and I am crying because I don't feel guilty, and I don't feel alone. I feel like I am at the start of something wild and unknown, something made of light and furious possibility, but I am sad, too, because in order to know this, to feel this amazing, impossible moment, I have to leave those who love me behind.

The plane rumbles to the runway. It surges and rattles and gathers speed.

And we are off.

Part 2:
London

3:20 a.m., Tuesday

Awake again as we churn through the crystalline dark.
Most of the plane seems to be asleep. Some seats still with
their little rectangles of screen blaring blue light. Caleb is
out, now. We're snuggled against each other's shoulders. It
took us awhile: two movies and a bunch of video games and
even the crossword puzzle in the airplane magazine before
we finally dozed off.

I twist to see Val, a few rows back, curled into a child-
sized ball, covered by a blanket except for the very top of
her head.

Outside, there is nothing but black and stars, and, if I
press my face against the glass, a red rim of moon setting
behind us.

I feel weirdly numb, headachey and dried out from the
airplane air, from a day spent barely eating and wringing
my insides out.

I click my screen back to life. Blue light on my face.
A tiny plane birthing a white line across a midnight blue
map. We are over Calgary. Catherine Summer Carlson is
in Canadian airspace, in the mountain standard time zone,
in the upper troposphere.

Back on the surface of the earth, in American airspace,
in the Pacific time zone, it is after two in the morning, and
my parents . . . could they possibly be sleeping? I doubt it.

More likely they are sitting on the couch, with glasses of

wine, furious, worried. Maybe Aunt Jeanine is there. Imagining it makes the adrenaline pistons fire in my gut, and my guts are so tired from the stress and worry. All I want to think about is what is ahead. Forward.

I keep telling myself that I'll be back in four days. And when I'm back they can punish me all they want. It will be worth it, right? And who knows? Maybe by the time I get back, they'll have come around. Maybe they'll have thought about what this meant for me . . .

Could that be how it goes?

Please?

I can't believe we're on this plane.

I switch to another movie. Some romantic comedy that involves dog-sitting.

We sail on through the dark.

1:34 p.m., GMT

Greenland!

Forehead pressed against the window. Stunning. Stunned.

Reykjavík on far too little sleep . . . The words, they sort of make sense, but only enough to make you feel like there is something wrong with your brain.

Also, you know, Vikings and stuff:

We barely speak in the Keflavik airport. Briefly pass out on a row of chairs. I gaze out the windows at a world of volcanic black covered by folds of emerald-green moss. Clouds gallop low overhead in a constant wind. A place that feels in flux, as unfinished as we are.

Swimming out of a haze, my head a soup of pinpricks, I gaze at my phone. Still in airplane mode. Still showing Los Angeles time. It would switch to local time if I activated the network or Wi-Fi, but then I might get a text, or a voice mail. My parents must have tried to contact me by now. . . .

I slide the phone back into my pocket. Our next flight boards in a half hour. Easier just to stare off at the volcanic hills.

Caleb reads a wrinkled guitar magazine. It seems to be a nonstop assault of advertisements and dudes with questionable hair.

"How can you read that?" I ask him, my head falling on his shoulder.

Caleb smiles. "You don't really read it. More like you wander through it and see what you connect with. Like, which pedals look cool, which guitars, what musicians look like people you'd find interesting."

"Which hairstyle you're going to get." I point at the sneering rocker in an amplifier ad, his hair teased up like my mom used to do in high school. "Don't you need to hear a guitar to know it's right for you?"

"Yeah, but appearance is part of it. I guess that sounds kind of shallow, but it's not. It's sort of like seeing someone you are attracted to—"

"Please don't compare women to guitars—"

He smiles. "I won't, not exactly. But what happens is, you see a guitar and you imagine yourself playing it. You picture the two of you together onstage. And like, when a guitar just looks like *you*, it's almost like the sound will probably be right, or you'll want to meet it halfway, or something. It's the same with pedals and amps. Oh, and also it's interesting to read about how these musicians spend their days and what their habits are and stuff."

"Like what vodka that dude puts in his cereal?" I'm pointing at another rocker, this one with a shaved head and plenty of tattoos.

"He's vegan," says Caleb. "The thing about most musicians is that they're totally OCD. Have to use the same guitar picks, have to wear the same gig underwear—"

"Gross!"

"I put vodka in my cereal one time," says Val.

We both look over. She's curled in her seat, drawing on her left Converse with a black fine-point Sharpie. "Lucky Charms," she adds, not looking up. "They're magically delicious!"

Caleb and I both search for something to say.

"Oh, stop," she says. "It wasn't for breakfast. And it wasn't recently." She continues sketching a series of airplane

102

tails along the white rim of her shoe.

"I can't believe you're doing that," says Caleb. "They're brand-new."

"I think it looks really cool," I say.

"This is part of *my* OCD musician thing," says Val. "I buy a new pair before any tour, and make it like a journal. It's cooler than taking pictures. I was doing a pair on our Chicago–Denver trip, not that you all would have noticed."

"Maybe that's because I couldn't see them around Matt's boner," says Caleb.

We all crack up.

"He misses you," I add.

"Yeah," she says like it can't be helped.

"You were just hooking up with him," Caleb says. "It wasn't more, was it?"

Val shrugs. She draws a tiny Icelandair logo on one of the airplane tails. "I didn't really consider it becoming anything more," she says. "He's a sweetie, but . . . I'd just let him down." A shadow passes over her face. "Well," she adds quickly, "you know, after I got him off."

We giggle again, and I'm so tired that it feels like soda bubbles behind my forehead, but I also notice that Val stops laughing far earlier than Caleb and me.

4:09 p.m.

"What are you doing?" I ask Caleb as I wake, halfway

103

through our second flight.

He's been typing on his phone since we took off.

"You didn't turn on the Wi-Fi, did you?"

"Nope." He passes me the phone. The notepad is open and there are words. It takes travel brain a minute to realize they're arranged in lines. Lyrics.

"How do they go?" I ask him.

He leans into my ear, his breath warm, and sings in a whisper:

I see the future and all I see is you
I've been making plans since you took my hand
But when you ask me, I keep it to myself
It's not the future, until you see it too

Let the miles come, it doesn't matter
Let the time zones change, it doesn't mean a thing
If you're where you want to be, I want to be there too
If you're where you want to be then . . . I'll be with you.

I mash my lips against his. "You are way too sweet," I say.

Caleb nuzzles his face against my neck. "I mean it. I feel like, if we can make it through this, we can make it through anything."

I hold him and wish these plane seats were more private. As we kiss again, I can practically feel Val rolling her eyes from three rows back, not that she can even really see us.

I sink back to sleep on Caleb's shoulder, trying to picture our future together, but my own future is still too foggy.

6:25 p.m.

It is dark by the time we land, so at first, London is just another airport anywhere.

We leave the plane and head directly for the gift shop across from the gate. We separate, stumbling around, and reconvene at the register. I put down trail mix and an energy drink. Val has a long package of plain-looking round cookies.

"What are those?" I ask.

"Biscuits," she says. "It's what you're supposed to do. Also these." She has a package of potato chips that are steak and onion flavored.

"Gross," I say.

"I know, right?" She grins big, but it's interrupted by a yawn.

Caleb arrives with a city map and three wristwatches. "Check these out," he says. They are cheap tourist trinkets, gold-colored watches on black faux leather bands, with the Union Jack on the face. "This way, we can leave our phones off the whole time," he says.

"I like the sound of that," I say.

Val unfolds the map and runs her fingers over the diagonal lines of the city. "This primitive technology is amazing."

"That will be nineteen pounds thirty," says the cashier, and I can tell we're all trying not to giggle at the awesomeness of her accent.

But then it hits me what she's saying. "Oh," I say, "we only have . . . Do you take American dollars?"

The woman just gazes at us. "There's an exchange booth that way."

"Can we leave this stuff here?" Caleb asks.

The cashier just sighs and sweeps it all into a bag that she stashes beside her.

"How much cash do we have left?" Val asks as we walk through the terminal.

I carefully remove the envelope from my bag and thumb through. "Six hundred and some change," I say. Moments later, I hand it over to an expressionless young man in a suit vest, and after he makes the conversion and extracts a convenience fee, we are handed back a pile of notes and coins that is just over four hundred pounds.

"Is that enough for the week?" Val asks as we walk back to the gift shop. "I've heard London is expensive."

I shrug. "We're going to have to make it last," I say. "I have my parents' emergency credit card but if I use that, it might as well be for a plane ticket to Nepal, since they would kill me."

"Aren't they already going to kill you?" Val asks. "I'm not saying you should use it . . ."

"I just . . ." Somehow the idea of using that card seems

like a huge betrayal. As if coming here wasn't enough of one. "Let's just get to the youth hostel and pay for our nights, then we'll split up the rest of the money and eat cheap."

We get our supplies and make our way to the Tube. It takes us an hour to get to London proper, on a train filled mostly with arriving tourists. There are locals, I think, too, and if my senses weren't like a smooth-sanded stone right now I would probably be noticing interesting details about this new world, but mainly I'm staring blankly at the ads on the walls.

"How are you doing?" I ask Caleb.

He shrugs. "Somewhere between fine and completely losing my head," he says.

"Do you want to go to Eli's apartment tonight?" Val asks. "The hostel is pretty close."

"No," says Caleb. "Let's sleep. I couldn't handle that tonight."

We get off the train at Piccadilly Circus and make our way up to the street. London bustles around us, its streets arcing away in irregular curves. Throngs of people cross the wide plaza at all angles. Black taxis whir by, and we see our first actual double-decker bus, wonderfully historical and yet sleek and modern. The night swirls with the lights, and the horns, and voices.

It takes us a few wrong turns to get oriented, and it is immediately obvious that compass directions will be of little use here. Caleb is buried in our little map, using his phone flashlight. "I think if we turn right . . . maybe?"

We walk in exactly the wrong direction for a while, but eventually we make it to the hostel. The guy at the front desk is named Teddy. He's a couple years older than us, with bleached hair and excellent tattoos. He takes twenty-two pounds per person per night, and shows us to the single-sex dorm rooms. We get a quick look at the spare metal-frame beds, hear the snores already droning away, and decide we need a few more hours to wind down.

"There's some food left down in the café," Teddy tells us. "Stew. Free of charge as it's been sitting on the counter for a few hours. Still perfectly good though. I'll get you some?"

"Definitely," I say. We follow him to the kitchen and sit at a long table. It's just us and a quartet of girls slightly older than us. They are at the table behind us, drinking tea and talking loudly with a map between them.

"I just felt like," says one of the girls, "when we were in the Globe, I don't know . . . it's like I *was* Juliet, Helena, Ophelia. It was so . . . intoxicating."

I glance at Val and she rolls her eyes.

"Here we are," says Teddy. "Stew and bread. You want pints with that?"

I glance at Caleb and Val.

"Yes," says Caleb immediately, "yes we do."

"I'm good, thanks," Val adds, frowning. When Teddy leaves, she adds, "Don't enjoy those too much in front of me, okay?"

We sip our beers and eat stew. With each bite, I feel sleep dragging me down.

Behind us, the girls chatter on.

"I think Shakespeare would have been a very attentive lover."

The girls burst into wild laughter. One of them catches me glancing back. "Sorry," she says, sounding very American, her face red. "This is what happens when you let a bunch of lit majors loose in London."

It occurs to me that, in just a year or two, college me could be here, or somewhere, doing this kind of thing.

And without betraying my parents!

A voice inside wonders if I really had to betray them now.

But yeah, I really did.

The heavy stew and beer barge through my last defenses, and the pure exhaustion of these last few days starts to drag at my eyelids.

"I think I need to call it a night," I say.

"Yeah," says Caleb, yawning.

"I'm going to wind down for a little longer," says Val as we stand.

Caleb checks his tourist watch. "So, let's meet by the front door at . . . nine?"

"Affirmative," says Val.

Caleb and I stumble upstairs, holding hands. "I wish we were sleeping in the same place," Caleb says as we reach the hallway intersection.

"Oh *do* you?" I press up against him.

"Just to sleep," he says, "I swear."

"I don't," I say, putting my face against his neck. "But I am so, so tired. You can dream about me while you're sleeping with a bunch of dudes."

"At least our parents would approve of our sleeping arrangements," Caleb says. We kiss more, and then he squeezes me. "No matter what we find, it means everything to me that we did this, that you would believe in doing this."

I nod against him. We kiss sleepily, and I fight off the urge to crawl inside his skin. Pull away . . . Push him toward his dorm. "Good night."

I use the bathroom, then pick my way across the dorm to my assigned bed. With the snoring, the only way to sleep is going to be with earbuds in. I set my music to shuffle, take off my hoodie and jeans, and tuck into the narrow twin bed.

Orange streetlight draws trapezoids on the walls. I feel like I should consider where I am, just how far away I've traveled and why that feels as lonely as it does exciting . . .

But sleep has me in moments.

6:55 a.m., Wednesday

I'm awake by seven, like it or not. Bedsprings are sighing and floorboards are creaking all around me as everyone

110

rises for busy days being tourists. When I finally sit up at eight, I look around and realize that Val is not among us. It doesn't surprise me. What would, with Val? I think of her sitting down there in the café when we left her last night, and imagine all kinds of scenarios. Teddy was an obvious target for Val's interest. Or a late-night walk where, knowing her, she'd find a club or a party or something.

I tie my hair back, take a shower, and head downstairs.

Val is asleep in an easy chair in the living room. People bustle around her, drinking tea, consulting maps. She's oblivious to it all. I head down to the café and get us a scone to split, fix two cups of the complimentary tea, and place them on the table beside her.

"Val," I say, shaking her arm gently.

"Mmm." She half opens an eye at me. "It's not nine yet."

"Well, no. I got you a tea, and if you wanted a shower or something . . ."

Val scowls. "What are you trying to say?" She turns and scrunches herself into the corner of the chair.

"Your friend and I were up chatting pretty late." Teddy is stepping out from behind the desk and walking over. "When she finally fell asleep I didn't have the heart to wake her."

"Oh, okay," I say.

"Don't worry, I had my eye on her," said Teddy.

I look up at him, mostly trying to get my half-awake brain to process what he's saying.

Teddy rolls his eyes. "*Not* like that."

"Oh, I . . . Sorry."

"Quite all right," says Teddy. "This is a pretty plum job for meeting the ladies, I'll admit." He holds up his hand and I see a wedding band. "Honestly, all that would be exhausting, never mind not at all cool. Your mate and I did chat though. She showed me the address you guys were going to check out." He holds out a scrap of notebook paper. "London's twisty. I drew you a little map."

"Oh, cool. Thanks."

Teddy must see the worry on my face. "She told me why you're here," he says, "about your sick step-cousin. Tragic. It's really nice of you to come all this way to visit."

"Yeah," I say. Not bad, Val! "We needed to be here for her."

"I never would have pegged you two for sisters," says Teddy.

"Half sisters," I say quickly, holding back a smile. "We're pretty different."

New arrivals ring the bell on Teddy's desk.

"Well, good luck today," he says, and heads back.

"You're good," I say quietly to Val.

She sits up and rolls her eyes. "Lot of good it did me. I thought I had him, but then he has to go and be married."

"Scratch that. You're terrible."

"The terriblest."

Caleb comes down the stairs and spots us. "Hey," he

112

says, giving me a kiss. "How was your night? Did you sleep?"

"Some of us more than others," I say.

Caleb glances at Val. "Oh no, you didn't."

"No," says Val. "But not for lack of trying. Had to do something to take my mind off things."

"How about you?" I ask Caleb.

He shakes his head. "I must have slept, but I barely remember it." He glances nervously toward the window. "So . . . we ready?"

"Are you?" I ask him.

"No," he says, "but let's go."

Val slugs down her tea and the piece of scone. "Time to go find Dad!" she says, the enthusiasm oh-so-fake.

I'm reminded that while I've thought a lot about how this will be for Caleb, to confront the dad who abandoned him, Eli has no idea that Val even exists, does he?

How exactly is that going to go?

But then, if Eli researched enough to know about Caleb and the band's trip to New York, he might have figured it out about Val.

Or, it's going to completely blindside him.

It's a cool, misty morning. We make our way down crowded sidewalks, along winding streets, through trapezoidal intersections. The streets teem with cabs, double-deckers, and cars that are comically tiny by American standards. The gray and white and brick buildings

113

really do evoke a sensation of history that inhabits you, as if this city is a bleeding border where multiple eras still exist simultaneously. There is something immediate about London: the sounds and bustle and the cloak of low clouds, the sameness of streets over hundreds of years old. It makes you believe in past lives, in reincarnation, in magic and shadows. Around the bend of each canal or alley . . . doorways and moorings, gateways to lands exotic and far and all of this seems to be in the very molecules you breathe.

Los Angeles reinvents itself on a daily basis, always focused on what's next. There is no past, no history, or if there is, it's only because that block hasn't sold yet.

This place *is* history.

After about ten minutes, we are turning down Frith Street. It's quieter, narrow, lined by white and brown brick buildings with shops on the ground floor and two stories of flats above.

"It's just up here," says Val, reading the map and the numbers on the doors.

Caleb has gone silent. I squeeze his hand. It is cool with sweat. "You can do it," I say to him. "Do you know what you'll say?"

"After *Hey, Dad?* No clue, really."

Val stops in front of a shoe store with an all-glass front. She points to the door to the side.

"This is it."

A white painted door with a tarnished brass knob.
A small sign taped to the inside of the glass.

Flat for Rent 3/1. Inquire within.

"You ready?" I ask, squeezing Caleb's hand.

"No, but here we are."

"Lead the way," Val says to him.

Caleb swallows hard and grasps the handle. The door is unlocked . . . maybe so potential renters can get in. We head upstairs.

It's a narrow staircase. The whole thing on a slight angle. Each step whines and creaks. We reach the landing for the second floor, turn, and head up to the third.

My heart is hammering and he's not even my dad. Is Eli White at the top of these steps? The human, the dead man, the myth, will he be up here watching TV, sipping coffee, strumming a guitar? Whatever he's been doing each morning for the past sixteen years?

We reach the top of the stairs. The door to the flat is open, to welcome prospective renters.

I rub Caleb's back. He breathes deep. . . .

Val steps around him and peers in. "Shit." She pushes open the door and we follow her in.

It's empty.

Dusty hardwood floors, a single floor lamp, its cord snaking to the wall. The windows are open, breeze blowing in. I recognize them from the second videotape, when Eli referred to his summer Soho sessions and we thought he meant New York.

The place smells like disinfectant.

"We just missed him," says Caleb. He stands there in shock. Val crouches down and runs her finger over a long rectangle of dust on the floor. The ghostprint of a couch.

I don't want this to be true. Need this to somehow not be true, and yet there is no changing the reality in front of us, the emptiness.

After all this, we were still too late.

"Be right there!"

It's a woman's voice coming from behind the bar that separates the narrow kitchen from the living room. It's a studio, with only a door into a small bathroom. I recognize the sound of scrubbing. Caleb and Val seem too stunned to move so I cross the room, my steps echoing off the bare surfaces, and peer around the bar.

An older woman is bent over the oven, scrubbing vigorously at the inside.

"I'll be just another moment," she says breathlessly.

Her hair is steel and white, tied back in a ponytail, a bandanna on her forehead. She's dressed like she's twenty: faded jeans over square-toed boots, a gray concert shirt with black three-quarter sleeves. The print on the back is too far gone to know what band it is.

She leans back with a sigh, wipes her brow on her sleeve.

She wears pink rubber gloves. She turns to me, drops the scrubber in a bucket of soap, and looks me over.

"Name's Susan. You're here about the flat."

"We . . . sorta?"

Susan's gaze stays on us for moment, then she nods, as if I've answered some big question for her. "I'd ask what you're doing here instead of being at school," she says, "but in your case, especially given your accent, I'm guessing that's a bit of a long answer."

It sounds like she might also mean something more. And the way she's looking at me . . .

But she stands and pulls off the gloves. "Old tenant moved out early," she says, businesslike. "Just yesterday, in fact." The front of her shirt says *The Kinks*.

She glances past me. "Thinking of splitting the place among three? It could be a little cozy." She smiles and steps around me, patting my shoulder as she does.

"How are you," she says, extending a hand to Caleb, then Val. She looks around, holding out her hands. "It's not much, but the bones are good. Solid plumbing. Better hot water than you could expect for this part of town."

"We're not really here about renting the place," says Caleb.

"I gathered." Susan looks out the windows for a moment, in thought. "I told him there was no rush," she says, her tone suddenly serious, "but you know how sometimes you feel like you gotta do something, and you can't rest until you do."

117

"We're familiar with that," says Val.

"Did you . . . know him?" Caleb asks tentatively.

"The tenant?" says Susan. "Of course I did. Mr. Walsh has been renting here since I still lived downstairs with my bastard ex-husband."

"Mr. . . . Walsh," I say. "Was that his real name?"

Susan makes a face that is sort of a smile and sort of a grimace. But what I am sure it tells me is that she definitely knows. She knows what we're *really* talking about. But why is she being cryptic about it?

"If he had another name, I didn't need to know it," she says. "He always paid in cash, and always on time. I never saw the need to do a background check or any of those unseemly things."

"Where is he now?" Val asks.

Susan shrugs. "It's not my business to know my tenant's plans. Long as they pay me on time and keep my places tidy, I keep out of their business. I rent five flats around town and I don't let it get personal. Mr. Walsh didn't tell me his plans and I didn't ask. Now, would you like a tour of the place?"

"We don't want a tour!" Caleb suddenly snaps.

"Hey," I say, putting my arm around him. He feels so tense, every muscle pulled tight. "It's okay. We'll figure this out." I try to tell him with my eyes that we're good here. That even though Susan is being cryptic, she knows what we want to know and I'm pretty sure she wants to tell us more . . .

118

If we can only figure out what's holding her back.

"I understand. Believe me, I do," says Susan, "but I'd sure like to show you the place so you have the proper feel for it."

"I'm sick of these games," says Caleb. "We . . ."

"Caleb," says Val.

He doesn't finish, trying to get control of himself.

But Val turns to Susan. "We didn't come all this way to be played with."

Susan's eyes fall for a moment. She glances at the window again, and then speaks softly. "Did it ever occur to you that maybe you're not playing a game? That maybe, this is all very serious."

"You think we don't know this is serious?" says Val.

"I think . . . ," says Susan, "that if you let me show you the flat, you might find things more to your liking."

Caleb shrugs. "Okay, but . . . what else is there even to see?"

"You'd be surprised," Susan says.

"Guys," I say, "let's just take a look, okay?"

"Your call," says Val.

"Fine," says Caleb.

Susan points us to the bathroom. "Pretty standard," she says. "I'm going to update a couple things this week. Let me show you the kitchen."

As she crosses the flat, she adds, "Now, I don't want to pressure you, but I have had other interested parties. One in particular stopped by this very morning, and I think he's anxious to move in. I'd rather rent to someone young like yourselves, but he did make a very serious offer."

Caleb and Val and I share a glance. It seems like we're supposed to be getting some hidden meaning from that, but what?

Susan steps into the kitchen. "As you can see, not much space but very functional." Then she sighs almost theatrically. "Oh, would you look at that."

She reaches up on top of the refrigerator. Something's lying there. "Mr. Walsh will be very disappointed that he left this behind."

Susan holds out a flat cardboard square.

A record.

The sleeve is rough cardboard: a Pink Floyd album titled *Reaction in G.*

"This is an extremely rare bootleg," says Susan, "especially a vinyl pressing." She hands it to Caleb.

"I thought you said this was Mr. Walsh's?" he says, eyeing her.

"I also said that I don't have any idea where he's gone, and I need this place cleaned out. Why don't you take it? It will be a nice souvenir for you. Or, if you need funds for the rest of your trip, it would fetch you a good price."

Caleb holds the record in both hands. He looks like he might just break it, or toss it out the window. "What are we supposed to do with this?"

"I'm not sure," says Susan.

"You're lying," says Val.

"Mmm, it would be more accurate to say that I am being selective in what I say." She crosses over to the windows, steps into the shadow beside them, and peers out. "Believe me, it's as much for my protection as for yours."

Val and I take that as an invitation. We join her and look out, too.

"End of the block," she says. "Silver BMW."

I find the car. And the two men standing beside it. There is an older man with wavy white hair, wearing a white shirt and a dark tie and pants. Beside him is a tall, much thinner man, bald, with small oval glasses. Even from this distance, I know him. He's not someone I'd easily forget.

"Oh hell." Val leaps back from the window.

I step back slowly. I'm pretty sure they're too far away to see us but I still don't want to do anything to attract attention.

"That's the other interested party I mentioned," says Susan. "I gather you know them."

I turn to Caleb. "It's Kellen."

Caleb's face goes pale.

"I don't know who the other guy is," I say.

"He's Detective Ames from Scotland Yard," says Susan. "He didn't say a word while they were here, but the badge on his belt was hard to miss."

Val whistles. "Holy crap, Scotland Yard . . . Are you

121

kidding me? I did not sign up for a bout with Sherlock Holmes."

My throat feels tight. My mouth dry, hands clammy. And maybe I'm going to pass out.

Susan puts a hand on my shoulder. "It's okay, hon. Those men out there had some pretty specific questions about my former tenant, but like I said, I didn't know much about him. And they didn't ask me anything about other prospective renters, if you catch my meaning."

I nod. "Sure, but we walked right by there on our way here." I feel like I'm about to vomit. I hug Caleb. He is stunned silent.

Susan points to the record. "Take that keepsake, I believe it will give you some answers. When you leave, head out the window on the landing. There's a fire escape that leads down to the alley. Here's my card. In case you need help with that record."

"Thanks," I say to Susan, taking her card and slipping it into my pocket.

"We need to go," says Val.

"Why can't you tell us more?" Caleb asks, even as we are turning to leave.

"I honestly don't know any more," she says. "But I also believe that the dead deserve our discretion."

If there were even the slightest question left about whether we were, in fact, talking about the same person, that pretty much confirmed it.

We hurry out of Eli's old flat. I snap a picture of those windows, sunlight streaming in. We nearly run down the stairs to the landing, and Val yanks open the window. We scramble onto the fire escape, hurry down to the end, then drop to the alley. It's all mostly terrifying.

"I'm not exactly feeling the thrill of international intrigue," I say as we hurry up the alley in the opposite direction from Kellen.

"Maybe that kicks in once the pure cold panic wears off," says Caleb.

Somehow I doubt it. We're a couple blocks away before I can even think straight.

10:22 a.m.

"We are screwed," says Val.

We're sitting on a park bench about ten fast-walking minutes from Eli's old flat.

"How did he find Eli? Now, after all this time?" I wonder.

"Maybe he's been following us?" Val suggests.

I'm staring at my phone. Still in airplane mode. What would I find if I turned it on now? Has Scotland Yard been trying to reach us? Have they been in touch with my parents? If they figure out who we are . . . forget that we're looking for Eli. We took Val out of the country. That's likely some kind of crime. Could it be like an Amber Alert?

She is under eighteen. . . .

Once again, I slide my phone back into my pocket, unchecked. I don't want to know. Can't risk knowing, at this point. I'm overcome by the feeling that I really just want to be home.

"Jerrod wouldn't have told Kellen," I say, trying to calm down and think it through. "Jerrod's been keeping Eli's secret from *everyone*."

"Maybe it was Eli's trip to New York," says Caleb. "Maybe Kellen got word of that somehow. Whatever, it doesn't matter now. This must be why Eli moved out early. Maybe Jerrod knew Kellen was coming, and tipped Eli off. Or maybe Eli left early because he somehow found out that we were coming. Uhhh." He bangs his head against the record. "My brain is broken."

"Let me see that," I say, taking the square of weathered cardboard. "Susan made it seem like Eli left this for us. It must be a clue of some kind about where we can find him." I turn the record over, reading the credits. "This is the original Pink Floyd lineup," I say. "A live bootleg recorded in Copenhagen in 1967."

"What kind of message are we supposed to get from that?" Val asks.

"No idea, but it's a pretty cool relic." I pull out the vinyl, along with its dust jacket. The edges of the cardboard are worn to white, and the paper sleeve has a corner ripped off. This music, this copy, has history, a tactile connection to those who listened to it before. What living rooms has it inhabited? Whose ears heard it? And what were they thinking, drinking, who were they with? It occurs to me that there is no artifact anymore in our world. When I buy music on my phone it has no connection to others. No hands are involved; granted as soon as we listen and share with others, we make community, but the object is no longer a connecter. And sure, this record smells weird, and probably has scratches and skips, but there is still something tingly about holding it in my hands, and connecting to its shared history through its texture.

Also, there's something written on the plain white paper around the record.

"Is that *Mr. Walsh's* handwriting?" Caleb asks. We've seen Eli's writing before, in torn-out pages from his journal. This looks different. But the other notes were ones that he wrote sixteen years ago. This one was written . . . maybe yesterday? His writing could have changed.

It's wild to think that Eli might have been holding this record in his hand so recently . . . and yet he's still just beyond our reach. But maybe not by much:

Where Her Majesty was set free
Where She made her first Million
When they tell you you can't live your LIFE
Thursday
See you there, just like the Piper

The word *life* is circled. Actually it's not a circle. There are dash marks around the inner rim of the shape.

"That looks like a clock face," says Val, leaning over.

"How very Eli to pick that lyric," mutters Caleb. "What do you think it means?"

I turn back to the album jacket. "There's a song called 'One in a Million' on the record. This is maybe a lyric?"

"Maybe the clock face means the time when the lyric happens," says Val. "Like what time in the song. Maybe it's a time Eli wants us to know."

"When we're supposed to meet him on Thursday?"

"How exactly are we going to listen to it?" says Caleb. "I sort of doubt our hostel has a turntable." Then he elbows Val. "Maybe *Teddy* has one at his house." It's the closest to a smile he's come all morning.

I remember what Susan said as we left. If we needed any help . . . I dig into my pocket and pull out her card. "Check this out."

In the rush to leave the flat, I didn't even look at it, just assuming it was for her property management. But it's not:

Berwick Street Records
Susan Hopkin: Owner
M–F 12–9.

"Maybe she wants us to come find her," I say, tapping the record.

126

Caleb looks for the address on his map. "It's close by," he says, then he looks at his British flag watch. "What are we supposed to do until noon?"

Val shrugs. "Kill time being tourists? We are in freakin' London. How about Big Ben and stuff?"

"Good plan," I say. "That might take our minds off things. Or at least make time move a little more quickly."

We head south. The rain has lightened up. We get toasted cheese sandwiches from a cart, and soon find ourselves in Trafalgar Square. Tourists teem around us. We eat on the steps of the National Gallery, watching the traffic spiral around a tall statue.

"Who is that supposed to be?" Val wonders.

Caleb checks the map. "Admiral Horatio Nelson," he says. "Died in the Battle of Trafalgar, 1805, which was—"

"Don't bore me with reality," says Val.

"I think the TARDIS landed here in the fiftieth anniversary special," I say.

"They should build a statue to that," says Val.

"Somewhere a roomful of British historians are choking on their tweed," says Caleb.

We've made it a little while . . . but now a silence falls over us, and worried thoughts return.

So we keep moving: Whitehall to Big Ben, a venture out over the Thames to look at the Eye, a trek through St. James's Park to Buckingham Palace.

We walk in the crowds, making the same route that

everyone out in London today seems to be making, cameras held out in front of them as they go.

It seems like we spend more time sidestepping and ducking around groups and couples taking selfies (which Val takes special pleasure in photobombing) than we do actually looking at the sights around us, and yet I find the crowds comforting. We will be nearly impossible to spot, for whoever might be looking for us.

Val and I are almost into it, letting ourselves make jokes and feel like we are tourists. Caleb has moments when he seems like he's here with us, but mostly he's quiet.

When we get to the palace, Caleb and I pose by one of the guards, but none of the silly poses we make can get him to break his serious face.

Val hands back my phone and says, "That note on the record. Eli mentioned 'Her Majesty.' Any chance that he wants to meet us here?"

I look around at the throngs passing by. "I don't know. It's too visible, I think."

"Maybe that's the point," says Val. "No one would suspect."

We linger for a little while, and when no mysterious strangers approach us, we start back through the park, on our way to the record store.

Caleb is quiet. "Want to talk?" I ask him as we cross over a meandering pond that is dotted with swans.

"I just can't believe he's still making us chase him," says

Caleb. He checks his watch. "Forty-eight hours from now we'll be on a plane home. And with Kellen here . . . It all just makes me more furious with him than ever. I almost wish we didn't come."

"We're close, though," I say. "We might still pull this off."

"I know." He squeezes my hand. "I'm doing my best to remember that." But it's hard, I can tell, and part of me thinks he's right. Just think of all the trouble we could *not* be in if we'd just stayed home, just let this go. But if there's one thing that makes me and Caleb and Val alike, it's that letting go with ease has never been our style.

12:09 p.m.

Berwick Street Records isn't too busy at noon on a weekday, but it's still alive with people thumbing through stacks and reading labels to one another. The listening stations are full of listeners bopping their heads, so we queue up nearby. CDs line the walls, while bins of vinyl dominate the center of the store. There are posters along the top of the wall and on the ceiling, T-shirts and other memorabilia pinned all around.

We've been waiting about five minutes when I spy Susan emerging from the back room. I wave and get her attention.

"Well, there are my prospective tenants," she says with a smile. Her wavy hair is down now, and she's wearing hip glasses. "Sorry about the act back at the flat, but it's easy to be paranoid. With something this sensitive, you can never be too sure who might be listening." She smiles warmly at Caleb and Val, and a look flashes across her face like she might cry. "I can see him in you both."

They both squirm a little at this.

"So," she says, glancing at the record. "Do we need to give that a spin? We've got a turntable downstairs with some vintage speakers."

We follow Susan into the back offices, and down a narrow staircase. There's a makeshift lounge set up: three couches and a stereo system, surrounded by walls made of stacked cardboard boxes.

"Did Eli tell you we were coming?" Caleb asks. "Sorry, Mr. Walsh."

"It's okay to call him Eli down here," says Susan. "He told me very little, in case he ever got found out. He didn't want me to get in trouble. He never even officially told me who he was, but I figured it out. He looked familiar to me from the day he arrived, and I didn't even have to search beyond the record store stacks to put two and two together.

"When he got back from his trip to Glasgow last week he told me he was moving out. He said he'd be out by Friday, but then yesterday he said he'd be gone by midnight. I'm assuming it was because of his old band mate showing up."

"You knew who that was," I say.

"I know how to do a Google search, yes."

"Eli didn't got to Glasgow," I add. "He came to New York."

"Ah. Because you were there for the pop festival." She winks at me. "I follow Dangerheart's activities, too."

"He told you about us?"

"Well, no," Susan says, "but I read the music sites, and word of who you were made a pretty big splash last fall."

Susan takes the Pink Floyd record and slides out the vinyl. "Eli told me to give this to the right visitors, and that he was sorry but he had to stay cautious. I was pretty sure I knew who he meant." She hands the sleeve back to Caleb and puts the record on. "Ready?" she asks, picking up the needle.

"Ready," says Caleb.

The needle pops and hisses in a repeating pattern. The speakers breathe like it is going to be loud, and when it begins, the sound seems brown and warm and knife-edged. Volume overwhelms the space and the raw live track swallows us like the maw of some ravenous creature.

The guitars scream. The drums bash. The whole song hums and warbles and vibrates. By any modern standards it's a poor-quality recording. But as a bootleg from a small club more than forty years ago . . . it has this undeniable energy, primal, like something ancient clawing its way to life. You can almost hear the sound hitting the walls in that room, feel the air that the amplifiers are pushing. It sounds like what *being* at a show is actually like.

"'Reaction in G,'" says Susan, reading off the track listing. "This is a song about how much they hated playing their first hit single."

"I don't hear any words," says Caleb.

"That's part of their reaction," says Susan. "I remember seeing them do this in Liverpool once. It was so strange. And so captivating."

"You saw Pink Floyd in 1967?"

"I saw all the bands back in the day. It wasn't even that big a deal. Going to see Floyd or the Who was like if someone came to see Dangerheart at that Holiday Meltdown you played a few months ago."

"I'd say it's pretty different."

"Give it forty years," she says. "Maybe people will be passing around bootlegs of your shows."

When Syd Barrett starts to sing on the next track, it's so distorted and maxed out, you can barely decipher the words.

"These guys are terrifying," says Val, smiling big.

"What was more terrifying was trying to get them anywhere on time and sober," says Susan.

"Wait, you *worked* with them?" I ask.

Susan nods. "Briefly. I helped out with them, and a couple other bands. That was before I took a job with Apple Records."

"Were you a musician?" Caleb asks.

"Careful with your tense there, mister. Just because I'm

an older woman doesn't mean I exist in the past tense. I still play guitar, pretty darn well, but I didn't have the voice for a girl group, or like a Janis or someone, and rocker women like Joan Jett were still a decade away. So yes, I am a musician, but back then, no, I worked behind the scenes."

"That's cool," I say. This Susan woman is easily the most interesting lady of my parents' generation that I have ever met.

We swim through the artful noise of the next song, "Arnold Layne," and then "One in a Million" begins.

I realize the turntable doesn't have a time display. "I'll keep track of the time," I say, holding up my watch.

The song is a slow, dirty groove, psychedelic, I think it would be called. Menacing, but with a swagger that makes you want more. That said, we can barely make out the words.

"Here." Susan hands Caleb her tablet. She's pulled up the lyrics online. "If I remember right, that line you wanted is pretty hard to hear."

"Here it comes . . . ," says Caleb.

Syd Barrett screams: *"When they tell you you can't live your life . . ."* Barely audible over the smashing drums and screaming guitars.

"Pretty much exactly the one minute mark," I say.

We listen through the song and after it slams its way to the end, Susan picks up the needle.

"Okay . . . ," says Caleb. "So we're supposed to meet

him at one o'clock, tomorrow, but where?"

"He didn't tell me," says Susan.

"Did he leave anything else behind?" Val asks. "Or say anything else?"

Susan shakes her head. "I'm afraid not."

"It must be in this message," I say, running my finger over the scrawled lines. "What does he mean that Her Majesty was set free . . . ?"

"We were thinking Buckingham Palace," says Caleb, "which might be perfect because it's crowded or totally wrong because it's crowded. Hard to say."

Susan stands. "Let me think some more about it. We have a little time. At the moment, though, I need to set up for this afternoon's in-store show. You know, I could swap out that dust jacket, and you could sell that record for a nice price, if you need a little extra cash for this trip."

"That would be great," I say.

Susan finds another white paper dust jacket in a stack of albums by the stereo, and while she replaces the vinyl, I fold up the one with Eli's message and tuck it away.

We head upstairs and bring the record to Susan's associate, Derek. "Ooh, nice," he says, inspecting the record's condition. "Haven't seen one of these in a bit." He's wiry and covered in multicolored tattoos, wearing a T-shirt and jeans. He's sporting a finely trimmed beard and a bow tie around his bare neck.

He consults a weathered book on the back counter. "I

can give you guys forty pounds for it, if that works? It's rare, but not like *Sgt. Pepper* in mono or anything."

"We'll take it," I say.

"What are you doing with the rest of your day?" Susan asks as we're splitting up the money.

"Trying not to lose our minds," says Caleb.

Susan checks her phone. "The in-store is at three. A band from Manchester called the Poor Skeletons. They were actually supposed to be here by now to do a sound-check but their train is running late. Maybe you guys could be my soundcheck band instead?"

"Um," says Caleb, but he can't hide a grin. "It would be so nice to play. Except we don't have half our band."

"The Poor Skeletons are an acoustic trio," says Susan. "I'm only setting up for two guitars and a kick drum. Anything you could do with that arrangement?"

"Remember what we were messing around with a couple weeks back?" says Val. "That one time in rehearsal?"

"Oh yeah," I say, "that—"

Val holds a finger to her lips.

"If you have a couple acoustics," Caleb says to Susan, "we could maybe practice for a minute in the basement?"

"Sure," says Susan. "Let me get you set up."

As we head back to the basement, Caleb turns to me. "How's your foot-tapping ability?"

I nearly implode with stage fright. "I don't—"

"You can do it," says Val with a sly grin. "This is the

perfect place to fulfill your Yoko/Linda destiny."

"Shut up," I say, and yet, I allow a nervous smile as we head downstairs.

1:28 p.m.

We return to the main floor a half hour later, and things have completely changed. The area all around the front of the store is crowded with people, a mix of teens and hip twentysomethings. A line has formed outside the front windows, growing by the moment. Susan stands on a tiny triangle stage in the window. She has set up two mics and an old Gretsch bass drum with a sparkly teal coating.

"Umm . . . ," says Caleb, "so much for this just being a soundcheck."

"Come on, brother," says Val, slapping his shoulder, "this is way better than a soundcheck."

As we push our way to the stage, I can barely breathe. My part is very small, and yet, getting it wrong would ruin the song. The distraction of practicing has been just what we all needed, a welcome time away from all things Eli, but now I am really picturing being up there with all those eyes on me, and it is the opposite of what I ever want. I like to be at the side of the stage, at the back of the room, just beyond the lights, and yet I have to admit: in spite of the fear, there is also something magnetic about this idea of being not just in the music, but part of making it.

Caleb leans against me from behind and kisses the side of my neck. "You've got this. Just watch us and pin yourself to the quarter notes."

"Right," I say, but still, as we're stepping onto the stage, I am basically having a heart attack.

Val and Caleb assume their stage personalities, all business. They find the coiled cables on the floor and plug them into the pickups on their acoustics. I squeeze into the corner, behind the bass drum. My shoulder touches the cool window glass. The people in line outside are less than a foot away from me, some with their backs to the glass, others leaning in curiously, trying to assess their chances of getting a spot inside. I glance at the crowd milling in front of the stage and bristle at their quizzical gazes: sizing us up, deciding if they will make room among their tastes and opinions for us, whoever we are.

"You guys ready?" Susan asks.

Caleb checks back with me. I probably look like I'm going to barf, but I nod. "Pluto strong," says Caleb. "We got this."

I feel his confidence, and realize that while I've seen stage-Caleb a hundred times, I've never been with him in this exact moment, never felt the way that, once the lights are on and there's no turning back, he seems to emerge from the cloud of doubt that can so often swirl around him, and become a kind of energy source, radiating confidence and certainty. He *knows* he's got this, that he can own the moment, and while I've seen him pull it off so many times, I never realized just how strongly he exudes this power onstage. I want to let that confidence in, to be that *sure*, in the moments when it's most needed.

"Hello, everyone," Susan says into Caleb's mic. "The Poor Skeletons are held up on the Tube, but they should be here in time. Meanwhile, we've had a stroke of luck. A band from the States just so happened to be visiting our shop today, and are willing to help me do a proper soundcheck. So please give a warm Berwick Street welcome to Danger-heart, from Los Angeles!"

The crowd applauds politely, and eyes us curiously. My immediate urge is to read this look as skepticism, like they're waiting for us to fail. But I know that's just my nerves. I have to remember that when I've been in crowds for unexpected moments like this, I'm actually hopeful. For all our snarkiness and cynicism, we want to be impressed, want to discover something new, want to say we were there when *that thing* happened. And to be the ones who saw it first.

"Hey," Caleb says in the mic. "We're really glad to be here. This is . . . unexpected. At the risk of breaking unspoken rules, we're going to play the only song that we've really worked on as an acoustic trio. It's one of yours. So . . . be gentle with us."

This gets a laugh.

Caleb checks with Val, checks with me. We nod . . . and he starts the guitar riff.

It only takes a few notes before there is a murmur of recognition in the crowd. Most people's faces break into controlled smiles. There are also a few who cross their arms in "we'll see" formation.

Val lays into the strumming part. She nods to me and I gulp and start to pound the bass drum, my foot flexing on the pedal, stomping steadily and trying not to show how desperately I am counting along, trying to make sure that I stay in time. I watch Val's and Caleb's heads bob, their feet tap.

"Is this okay?" Caleb asks the crowd with a smile. It's the perfect endearing move, because here we are playing a song by the Beatles, in a London record store.

As Caleb and Val start to sing, the pulse of the bass drum becomes my everything. I am living beat to beat. I can barely hear Caleb and Val singing, partially because there is no monitor back here for me, but also because I am rooted to my part, to staying on top of it. I can barely look out at the crowd or I'll lose my focus, barely wonder all the normal things I'd be wondering about, how we sound and how we look and how the crowd is responding because any rival thought threatens the tenuous connection between my brain and my foot.

By now, many in the crowd are singing along. This is the kind of song that if you're going to play it, you have to nail it, and luckily, Caleb and Val have those complementary voices.

We're on our way home
We're going home . . .

They glance at each other as they sing, cracking into smiles. In my quick looks out into the crowd, I see their smiles returned, people nodding and bouncing along. A few in the arms-crossed set have already turned to their friends, saying something that elicits an affirming head nod.

A couple of them are still frowning.

But whatever! I can hear the gentle pitch of those singing along, feel the feet in the audience that are tapping along to my pulse.

It seems as if the song is over in seconds. The crowd applauds huge. We've won most of them over. I catch Susan's eye off to the side of the stage, and she nods, tears in her eyes.

"Play one of yours!" someone in the crowd calls. A guy near the front in a scarf and short-brimmed felt hat.

Caleb and Val share a glance. I move around from behind the drum. "You guys should do another one."

"You nailed the bass drum," says Val. "Don't you want to keep going?"

"Nah," I say, "I'm good." Actually that's such a lie. I want to be back here lost in the music forever. I have never known what it felt like to have a part in the music, to be on this side of the stage, behind the main speakers, just you and the thump from the amps beneath your feet.

But still . . . "That's enough rock stardom for this girl," I say.

I drop down to the side, standing with Susan by the little soundboard.

"Okay, we'll do a quick one," says Caleb. "This is called 'Starlight.'"

They play and I take photos from the side. An angle where Caleb and Val are in profile, and expectant faces look up at them, all with a halo of light through the store window, where more silhouettes watch. With each beat, each measure, I see the crowd nodding as they get to know the song, smiles breaking out here and there as it permeates their thoughts and sinks into their skin. It kills me that we don't have postcards or buttons or anything to give them, but then I tell myself, *Stop thinking! Just be here*. This moment feels meant to be, even better for its lack of planning.

Also, from this angle, I am reminded of what Susan said, because I can see the similar angle of Caleb's and Val's cheekbones. See the way their noses are alike.

When the song is over, the applause is even bigger.

"Thanks, you guys," says Caleb. "Stick around for the Poor Skeletons." He and Val unplug and step down as the crowd mills and murmurs. A few people shake their hands, compliment them as they make their way over to Susan and me. They are all smiles, breathless. I am, too, until my gaze wanders over their shoulders, and I spy a face at the back of the crowd.

It takes all my strength to keep my cool when I see Kellen standing by the door. His eyes meet mine and he nods, as if to say, *Yup, here I am.* I just stare, expressionless, and then look away slowly, and try not to seem rattled. Maybe it looks like I don't even recognize him.

I doubt it.

I turn toward the stage, and then Caleb arrives beside me, and we kiss, and when I check across the crowd again . . .

Kellen is already gone.

"Great job," Caleb is saying.

"Thanks," I barely get out, but I'm saved from having to speak further when the guy in the short-brimmed hat joins us.

"Guys, that was smashing." I see now that he has a guitar case in his hand. "I'm Dale from the Poor Skeletons. Really excellent stuff!"

"Thanks," says Caleb as they shake.

"How long are you in town for?" Dale asks.

"Just until Friday," says Caleb.

"Well, perfect. You guys should come to our show tonight at Bush Hall. We'll put you on the list. It should be a great night."

Caleb looks at me. I'm thinking we shouldn't be out late with our meeting tomorrow, but also that we are here and this is now and we should do all the things. I nod.

"Sounds really great," says Caleb.

"Definitely," Val agrees.

The crowd packs in around us, and we meet Jandy and Colin, the other members of the Poor Skeletons. They take the stage to huge, fervent applause. Their set is warm and nuanced, with the kind of easy songs that you find yourself singing along to by the end of each one.

I like them, but even so, my eyes keep drifting toward the door.

"What is it?" Caleb asks me at one point, when a song has ended and I'm virtually the only one who hasn't started clapping.

"Kellen," I say in his ear. "I saw him, watching us." Caleb looks around. "He left," I say. "But he definitely knows we're here and is watching every move we make. We're going to have to be twice as careful."

6:55 p.m.

We linger at Renegade after the Poor Skeletons' set, afraid to head back out on the streets, where Kellen might be lurking. Eventually, we can't avoid it, and we have business to get done: tea (I have to resist saying *Earl Grey, hot*), fish and chips, and then the computers back at the hostel, where we can do some much needed research.

I want to chat more with Susan before we go, but she's swamped with sales, with keeping the crowd orderly as the Poor Skeletons sign records. Just before we leave, I have

143

a thought and scribble it down on one of the Post-its she's using for signees' names.

"For later," I say.

Susan glances at the Post-it, then at me. And nods. "Sounds like a plan."

Actually getting out of there takes an extra minute because Val has targeted the Poor Skeletons' kick-drum-playing, tambourine-shaking percussionist who has an adorable mustache and impressive green eyes.

"Come on, killer," I say in her ear, tugging her away.

"No, please do stay?" she whispers in my ear. "He's Scottish. I'm done for."

"You'll just be cooler if you can leave now, then show up at his show later."

Val sees this wisdom in this.

We find tea and a chip shop, and then head for the hostel, where we wait until both computers are free.

"Okay, where to meet Eli," I say. "Let's start with the Copenhagen show."

"You don't think he really wants us to go to Denmark to find him by one o'clock tomorrow," says Val.

"He is running for his life, or his death, or whatever," says Caleb. "But no, it can't be that."

We read stories about the Pink Floyd show in question, but they don't lead to much.

"I'm looking at a discography," says Caleb. "'One in a Million' is sometimes called 'Rush in a Million.' Either way, it doesn't even appear on any of their major albums. It looks like they only ever played that song live."

"And we still don't think he means Buckingham Palace?" says Val. "Or maybe it's, like, where Princess Diana died?"

"Diana wasn't a queen, and she died in Paris," I say. "I don't know. Her Majesty . . . Why does that phrase still seem familiar to me?"

"Because it's a Beatles song," says Val, clicking.

"Ah, that's it," I say, remembering the letter that Eli left for us in Denver.

Val points at her screen. "Last track on *Abbey Road*."

"What does he mean by set free?" Caleb wonders. "Does she die in the song, or something?"

"Here are the lyrics . . . ," I say, clicking. "No, there aren't any references to dying or setting free, or to any places at all."

"It was cut, though, from the medley on side two of *Abbey Road*," says Val. "It was actually the world's first hidden track. So it was technically set free on that album."

"Are we supposed to find a copy of *Abbey Road*?" I wonder. "Makes sense with Eli's song title. Is there something in the two songs around it?"

"Maybe it has something to do with this 'where she made her first million' line."

"There's another song on this Pink Floyd list," says Caleb, scrolling. "It's called 'She's a Millionaire.' Also from

145

1967. It's also called 'She Was a Millionaire.'"

I do my own search for that. "Wait. Guys . . ."

There it is.

"Where Her Majesty was set free," I say. *"Where She made her first Million* . . . he means as in . . . first recorded. Pink Floyd recorded 'She's a Millionaire' in 1967 at Abbey Road Studios. Literally right down the hall from the Beatles."

"That's it!" says Caleb.

"Here's more: Pink Floyd recorded 'She's a Millionaire' while they were making their album called *The Piper at the Gates of Dawn.* Eli said *just like the Piper.* Okay. This has to be it."

"Abbey Road Studios," says Val. "So, what? Do we just show up there tomorrow at one?"

"I'm checking . . ." I load up the Abbey Road website. "It looks like the studio is still operating. I don't see anything here about tours . . . I guess we just go there and talk to the people at the entrance or whatever? Or maybe he'll just be waiting outside."

Caleb nods. "Unless he wrote this message before he realized Kellen was in town."

"This feels right," says Val, rubbing his shoulder. "I think this is it."

Caleb nods again. "It just better not be another dead end. Can we just fast-forward to tomorrow?"

"I wish," I say. "At least we have the show to go to. Let's clear these search histories."

We retreat to a couch in the common area, rather than going up to the dorm rooms. We all feel the best we have in days, and maybe that's why we crash so hard. Even I can't resist slipping into a brief nap. I wake up regretting it, though, feeling more fuzzy than before.

"We should probably rally if we're going to get to Bush Hall," says Caleb.

After another tea, I start to feel refreshed, and . . .

It's time to tell Caleb and Val that I have something else planned for the evening. Something small, but important.

"I wish you were coming," Caleb says as he and Val head down the steps.

"I'll definitely be there by ten," I say. "And if you're not there, I'll meet you back here."

"Oh, we'll still be there. We have a night on the town in London!" Val nearly shouts, bouncing on her toes.

"Okay. I'll miss you," Caleb says, blowing me a kiss.

"Yuck already," says Val.

"Watch out for Kellen," I say.

When they are gone, I sit on the front steps of the hostel, enjoying the fading evening light, the travelers arriving and departing around me.

Finally, my finger trembling, I slide off airplane mode.

I suppose I know why I'm finally checking. Given what I'm about to do, it makes sense.

My phone welcomes me "abroad!" with a message explaining about calling rates and such. And then texts begin to buzz in.

From late Monday:

Randy: Guys, are you all right? Everybody's worried sick. I know you want to find that third song but . . . well, I guess you've already gone so just be careful. Let me know what's going on.

Dad: Please let us know where you are and that you are safe.

From yesterday afternoon:

(424) 828-3710: You need to know that Kellen is on his way to London. I don't know how he found out about Eli. He doesn't know that I know. But he knows that you do. Watch out for him. And if he finds out about my connection, this will all be finished.

From last night:

Dad: We know you can take care of yourself. We just want to hear from you.

The texts from my father nearly crush me. He's writing to me so carefully, like his daughter is a drug addict, or suicidal, or a toddler at risk of another tantrum. It's obvious that he's holding so much back: anger, frustration, worry, and yet there is one thing his messages scream at me, and it is the one thing I realize I cannot take:

Guilt. I know I have my reasons for being here. Of

course I do. But my parents still have their hold on me. Part of me is still their little girl . . .

And suddenly all my walls crash down. I'm a puddle in moments, sobbing into my sleeve. It's not fair that I should have to make them so sad, just to be me. All I'm trying to do is find the larger truth of my life. Isn't it hard enough to believe in myself while I'm doing that? How am I also supposed to be responsible for the hopes and dreams of my parents?

I take a deep breath and type back, first to Randy:

Summer: We're good. Sorry we had to leave. But we're close! More soon, but don't worry. Actually stumbled into an in-store show today, so, woo hoo!

Then to my parents.

Summer: I am safe and doing fine. We are having an amazing time and finding what we need to find. I'll be back soon. I'm so sorry to disappoint you.

I hit send.

Slide the phone safely back into airplane mode.

Then I can breathe again.

Around me, it is twilight in London, the streets warming with light, people bustling about. I think about how I am in a foreign city, on an island, across a sea on a planet in space, and the great big world makes me smile and shiver at once, a feeling something like foolish wonder. A feeling that justifies maybe the worst part of how I feel about breaking my parents' hearts:

149

For this moment, and earlier today onstage, to be here, to be now:

It's worth it.

7:48 p.m.

"Hey." Susan is waiting for me at Oxford Circus, a fifteen-minute walk from the hostel. "I got you a chai. Do you want to sit or walk?"

"Walk," I say, still feeling restless, needing movement.

It's misting, heavy and windless and coating us in moments. We walk through crowds with collars upturned. The mist makes coronas around the streetlamps.

Susan lights a cigarette. "Don't ever start smoking these," she says, and then waves it at me with a smile. "Want one?"

"That's okay," I say.

"Good for you. So," says Susan. "You said you wanted to talk. Tell me your situation."

I give her the short and hopefully sane-sounding version: about college, about music. Two futures. Zero people happy about it.

"That sounds about right," she says. "I can certainly relate. For me, it was a band called the Go Static. I dropped out of high school my senior year to follow them on the road. I didn't want to miss a show, but I also wanted to convince them that they needed *me* to make it big. My friends called me a groupie, but they didn't get it. They didn't feel the way I did when I heard that band. Neither did my parents."

"I can certainly relate to all that," I say. "So your parents weren't happy?"

Susan laughs. "They were furious. My dad kicked me out of the house. I had to bunk in with my aunt and uncle for almost a year before I could afford to rent a room in a flat with three other ladies. Turned out my dad had been saving up for me to go to university. A little bit of every paycheck since the day I was born. He told me if I didn't finish secondary school that year, he'd transfer all the savings to my younger brother. That I'd never get another chance."

"Jeez. That's harsh. What did you do?"

Susan shrugs. "My dad never got it. That *was* my chance. I felt so sure. Besides, I'd never known he was saving for me. It was good of him to do, but it wasn't my choice. He had his dreams for me, and I had mine. I think you know a little something about this."

"Maybe a little. And then you worked for Apple Records?"

"Not at first," says Susan. "I was an unpaid assistant for a couple years, while working the late shift at a pub. They finally started to notice my work, and I got to work more closely with bands, manage tours. Those were amazing years. I'd never trade them."

"So what do you do now?"

"Well, I have the flats to manage and the record store

151

to run. The store also has a recording studio that I oversee. I produce the occasional band when I have time. And I still consult for Apple now and then when they need someone with an eye for how to build an artist. It's not the days of dressing right and hurrying around the office, but it still keeps me connected to the world, to people's ears. Now, tell me about you."

I hesitate, like I always do when it comes to talking about myself to another adult. But I remind myself that Susan is not Carlson Squared. She's not even Andre from Stanford. She's someone who already seems to understand more about me than anyone else except maybe Caleb.

"My parents just want what they think is best for me," I say. "They want me to go to college, to have a real career. And honestly, why don't I want that? Like, that's the part that sometimes I cannot figure out.

"They're actually sorta fine with music but they just can't deal with me not doing things the way you're supposed to. High school, college, the usual. I'll probably get in. And part of me wants to go, too. It's just . . . these things are happening *now*. Dangerheart just got signed, we're close to finding Eli, and it's all so exciting. My parents say there will be plenty of time in my twenties, but . . . I was feeling the other day like my whole life is already planned out and I know that's kind of ridiculous but sometimes it can feel that way."

We cross a busy intersection, and now Kensington

Gardens whispers darkly beside us: footsteps of walking couples, wheel turns of strollers, the flutter of fairy wings.

"A lot of people ask me if I wish I'd gone to university instead," says Susan.

"Do you?"

"Never for a minute. I mean, I'm sure something good would have happened, we all have multiple lives we could live, and many of them would make you happy. I figure there's really no one thing you're *supposed* to do, except the one thing that's truest to what you love. Just because something is expected, what *everybody* does, doesn't mean it's what you have to do. Here's an idea: Don't do the expected thing. Do *your* thing."

"That's what I feel like doing. But it's not going to be easy."

"It certainly won't. But I doubt your parents are as draconian as my father was. It's a different world now. Odds are, they'll get over it, and still support you even if you don't do exactly what they were hoping."

Hearing her words fills me with a nervous excitement, but I'm also getting overwhelmed by all the thoughts. "I probably just need to go home and take my punishment for this trip, first."

"Sure. Your parents are a little bit right, too, you know. About the future. I mean, here's the thing: in ten years, you're going to be okay. I know that about you, Summer, knew it after five minutes. But that cuts both ways. While you might be fine and have all the time in the world as an adult, you'll never be eighteen and have the chance to go off and be a freshman in college again. And you'll never be eighteen and be a part of a band that could go places. Both are adventures perfect for you, right now. Either one can happen. And, odds are, either one could happen again, in a not exact, but similar way, later on. In your twenties, your thirties. Hell, these days, in your forties or even fifties. What you have to do is decide which path feels most vital right now, in this moment, and follow that. It's probably hard, because I bet inside, your heart is screaming about both things."

"It's been doing a lot of screaming."

"Well, that's a good sign," says Susan. She makes a small salute with her cigarette before stamping it out on the concrete. Then she puts her hands in her pockets and we walk for a minute without speaking.

"So which do I do?" I ask.

Susan puts her arm around me and smiles. "I can't wait to find out."

8:19 p.m.

"We figured out where to meet Eli," I say to Susan. We're leaving the leafy border of the gardens, now making our way toward Bush Hall. I explain how we unraveled the details of the note, and how Abbey Road is our goal.

Susan gets out her phone. "I'm friends with the scheduling manager," she says while typing. "One o'clock is a pretty busy time of day at Abbey Road. I would assume he wants to meet you inside, as outside it will be mobbed with tourists, everyone taking pictures. I doubt Eli would want to put himself in the range of so many cameras." She taps a few more times. "I'm asking her if she can send me the schedule."

"We were thinking that was maybe just a starting point," I say. "And then he'll want to take us somewhere else." But I'm deflating, because what she's saying makes sense.

A little further into our walk, the schedule arrives. "All the studios will be booked solid," Susan reports. "Outside or inside, that's a lot of faces who could recognize Eli. It just doesn't sound like him. He's been so careful. . . ."

"It seems like what he meant, though." I pull the record sleeve out of my pocket.

"*See you there, just like the Piper . . .*," says Susan, reading over my shoulder.

"Yeah, the album Pink Floyd recorded at Abbey Road."

"Is it possible," Susan wonders, "that he meant be like the actual Piper in the title? As in . . ."

Suddenly I see it, too. "*Be at the gates of dawn.*"

"He might mean . . . ," says Susan.

"One a.m.," I say, "not one p.m."

"That would seem like a smarter plan to me on every possible level."

I check my watch. "Okay, wow. That's a lot sooner than we planned." My heart races. We should have time, but I still quicken my pace.

I can tell we're getting close to Bush Hall by the milling groups of people along the street.

A block before we arrive, Susan stops. "This is where I get off for the evening."

"You don't want to see the show?" I ask.

"I do," says Susan, "I just have too much work to catch up on. Plus, the later nightclub crowd can make me feel a little bit old. Come here. . . ."

She pulls me into a tight hug. Her coat is scratchy and damp. She smells like cigarettes. Somehow that is all so comforting.

"You have faith in what you truly feel inside, Summer," Susan says in my ear. "And if you ever need another walk-and-talk, you just give me a call, time zones be damned."

I pull back and find myself tearing up. "Thanks. Do you want us to let you know what happens tonight?"

"Sometime later," says Susan, pulling away. "When there aren't eyes on us."

"Okay. And thank you, Susan, for everything."

"You bet." She smiles and leaves. I watch her go for a moment, wiping my eyes, and then turn and head into the club.

I show my ID, I'm on the list, and in a minute I'm in. It's an excellent room. Ornately decorated with large mirrors along the walls, elegant chandeliers, and then a black-and-white tiled floor. Like something out of Alice in Wonderland, all lit in pinks and reds and with a band currently blaring from the stage. They play triumphant rock, and the front half of the floor is packed.

Most of the crowd is older, and I shake off a feeling of being exposed, as if everyone can somehow tell that I'm young and American and a deep disappointment to my parents.

Luckily I find Caleb down the far side of the room, leaning against the wall. He's got his hands in his pockets, his hair falling half in his face. He's watching the show, but something about his face makes me think he's actually lost in thought. Somehow, though, he senses me and he looks up and his eyes zero in. He smiles, just a little one that says "hey," but I can see that my presence has brought him back from wherever he was, lit him up inside, and I feel that happening inside me, too. He's also wearing a T-shirt that fits him great and damn, we need some alone time.

"How was your secret rendezvous!" he shouts into my ear when I hug him.

"Really cool! Just what I needed! You having a good time?"

"This band is loud!"

"Yes!"

Caleb shares his Coke with me, and we watch until the set break. We could be playing adult and having pints, but I can tell Caleb wants to be totally there.

"Poor Skeletons are up next," says Caleb. "We saw their soundcheck. They have full drums and bassist for tonight so it's a bigger sound. Pretty cool." He looks around the club. "We've got to play a room like this someday."

"Definitely." I scan the groups nearby. "Where's Val?"

"She was going to go see about getting a pint." Before I can respond he says, "And she informed me that she could control herself and that I had permission to come find her and drag her back if she was gone more than fifteen minutes."

I nod, always fighting that first, skeptical impulse. "We figured something out about Eli's note," I say, and explain the likely time change.

"Whoa," says Caleb. "So we probably shouldn't go to the after party that Dale invited us to."

"If we do we should keep a double-eye on Val," I say, "and stay away from the brownies."

"Yeah, no brownies."

Onstage, the Poor Skeletons are starting to set up.

"I'm going to use the bathroom," I say. "Be right back."

We kiss and I push my way through the crowd. The line for the bathroom takes ten minutes, and by the time I've gotten out of there, the Poor Skeletons have already started. The crowd on the main floor has grown, so I am threading and pushing my way through them. I'm working my way across in zigzags. It's when I make a wide move around a tightly packed group that my eye strays toward the bar.

I see Val.

I see Kellen.

They're talking.

He's leaning over her like a vulture, speaking into her ear.

I freeze. What the hell? But no, I need to trust Val. She doesn't know yet about the one a.m. time switch, does she? Unless she's already been back to check in with Caleb and then slipped away again.

As I'm stuck there, jostling between shoulders, Kellen stands up straight, pats Val on the shoulder. He hands her something small. A card? And then he slides away from the bar and straight toward the doors.

Val heads back toward Caleb.

I shove my way through the crowd and intercept her, grabbing her arm.

"Hey," I say.

"Oh, hey, you made it—"

"I saw you."

Val glances toward the door, and luckily doesn't try to deny it. "He cornered me over there," she says. "What a jerk."

"It looked like you guys were having a pretty in-depth conversation." I try not to sound mistrustful, but of course some of it is slipping in.

"Relax, Catherine," says Val. "I didn't tell him anything

except that we were signed to Candy Shell Records, and this was our celebratory trip. Pretty sure he didn't buy that at all, but whatever."

I want to believe her. I so, so do. But . . . "Does he know about Eli?"

"He told me that he's had a private-investigator service sifting through flight records and stuff for years, just in case. He said he never totally bought the suicide . . . And then Eli's name popped up last week for the NYC trip. I told him it could have been a different Eli, 'cause there's probably a bunch in the world, but he just smiled at that."

"Good try," I say.

"Yeah. I don't know how he figured out the flat thing. Maybe he asked my mom for any details that she remembered about being in London with him. Maybe he found the pictures like we did. Except she hates him almost as much as she hates Eli. And life. I don't know."

"So . . . ," I say. "He knows why we're here."

"Yeah. And he says he's got no issue with us, but obviously he does with Pops. Then he said a bunch of stuff about legal jargon and lawsuits and also me being a minor and blah blah." Val rolls her eyes. "Kellen's a serious dick."

"Did you tell him anything else?"

Val scowls. "Why would I tell him anything else?"

"I don't know," I say. "I'm just freaked out. This is all way too James Bond."

"Look, he wants us to help him but I told him to screw

160

off. I didn't admit to knowing Eli was here but obviously he thinks we do, so, tomorrow afternoon, we just have to be really careful not to lead that slimy over-the-hill rocker to my slimy undead father. Are you believing any of this? Or do you think I was actually plotting to join up with Kellen, find Eli, and be the new bassist on the Allegiance to North reunion casino tour?"

I bite my lip. "I don't think that."

"It's okay, I know you never totally trust me." She stalks off, back toward Caleb.

Tomorrow afternoon, she said. At least Val didn't even know the real meeting time when she talked to Kellen. But ugh, Summer, these thoughts! Not trusting Val, after all we've been through. I follow her back toward Caleb and I swallow it, yet, as the Poor Skeletons' set goes on, my eye is constantly darting to her.

I'm making fiction in my head. I know I am and I know it's stupid. But still . . . part of me thinks it's also stupid not to be at least a little worried. And another part of me thinks my brain is so wound up at this point I could make a conspiracy theory out of just about anything.

"What is it?" Caleb asks, leaning over. "Don't you like them?" He's been bopping up and down, totally into it, which I'm so happy to see.

"No, they're good," I say, and I resist telling him what's worrying me, and instead just focus on checking out the band. I can't wait for these hours to pass. I want to go now, to finally get our answers. We're so close! Just a little longer . . .

12:55 a.m., Thursday

The streets around Abbey Road are silent, a still life with only an occasional red bus chugging by. We cross the iconic white lines from the Beatles cover, sharing a smile with one another, but keeping quiet.

The building itself is unassuming, set back from the road, a sea of parking lot between its front door and the graffiti-scrawled outer wall. There are two gated entrances.

We watched the headliner at Bush Hall, and then got Indian food around the corner. Val sulked for a while about not having a chance to chat with the Scottish boy at the after party, and all the while I watched her with the slightest worried eye, that same old mistrust. Then we walked back to the hostel, stayed down at the café for forty minutes, and then, finally, made our way here, taking a zigzagging route, even doubling back at one point. And now . . .

We wait.

But with eyes peeled in either direction. Will it be a taxi, a car, a ghostly figure approaching out of the dark?

"It's one o'clock," Caleb finally announces.

There is a buzzing sound, and then with a rattle, the metal gate in front of the Abbey Road Studios parking lot begins to swing open.

"Do you think this is for us?" Val asks.

"I think we'd better find out."

We slip through, crossing the lot to the steps. The door buzzes when we reach it. Inside, a security guard gazes at us.

"Hi," I say nervously, "we're here to see—"

But he buzzes the inner door open. "Studio Two," he says.

We follow signs and enter a low-lit control room with couches on one wall and a large mixing console against the other.

"I'm glad you made it," says the woman standing at the board.

It's Susan.

We are too stunned to speak. She smiles and shrugs at the same time.

"I know," she says. "There are obviously some things I haven't been quite honest about."

"You . . . ," I begin, but I'm not sure what to say, trying to understand what it means that she is standing here now.

"What are you doing here?" Caleb asks.

"Running a recording session," says Susan. "I've been more than just your dad's landlady these last years. Wait, that sounds scandalous. It's not like that. What I mean is, I've also been part of his life. Okay, still not exactly what I mean . . ."

"Just tell us," says Val.

"Right." Susan breathes deep. "What I'm saying is, I help him . . . do this." She nods to the wide rectangular window above the console.

We all step toward it, until we can see through. The window looks down into a long, high-ceilinged room. There's only one light on inside. In the pool of light is a drum set, a bass, two electric guitars, and an acoustic, all perched on stands. Cords connect them to amplifiers whose orange standby lights glow. Sound baffles make artificial walls around the perimeter.

Sitting on a stool in the center . . .

It's him.

Eli.

The beard from New York is gone. His hair is a shaggy mop of brown, not unlike Caleb's but streaked with gray. He's wearing torn jeans and a flannel shirt, unbuttoned over a T-shirt.

Susan is pulling a large, round metal case from her bag. It looks like it should hold movie film.

"I'm also your dad's sponsor," she says. "We met in rehab. And this is our monthly meeting." She places the reel of tape down on a large, vintage machine, spooling the shimmering ribbon through. "We come here once every month, or more if he needs it. The scheduling manager and I go way back."

She hits a glowing yellow button and the tape spins into position. It makes a whir of sped-up sound, and then a few moments of a track play through the giant speakers. There's a guitar, and drums, and Eli's voice, and I'm certain this is a song that none of us have ever heard before. New material.

Down in the studio, Eli flinches at the sound coming out of his headphones. Susan hits stop. She moves to the control board and puts a finger on the studio microphone. Before she keys it, she turns back to us. "Just . . . don't say anything yet, okay? We sort of have a way of doing things, and he needs it to go that way."

The way she says it . . . Suddenly I understand something else, here in the dark.

Something that's going to hurt.

I take Caleb's hand and squeeze.

I don't even want to say it. Yet.

Susan speaks into a thin microphone. "How's everything?"

"Tuned and ready," Eli says in a mumble. Like any words he has to speak that aren't singing are a chore.

"Do you want to hear the takes from our last session?"

Eli is silent for a moment, staring down into a spot on the floor.

Seconds pass, three . . . four . . .

"No."

Susan sighs. "All right then, just a minute."

She turns back to the tape player, hits a series of buttons, and the tape begins to spin at high speed, but silent.

165

"What are you doing?" Val asks, stunned.

"Shh," Susan warns again. "I'm erasing the tape," she adds matter-of-factly.

"But do you have other copies of those songs?" Caleb asks.

Susan shakes her head. "No. Each time we get together, we tape, and then we listen back to the recordings, at least once, but usually two or three times. Then we record overdubs, sometimes for hours, until we get these pretty complete-feeling versions. And then Eli's one request is that I bring this same tape back to the next session, and if he says he wants to hear the tracks again, we'll listen. If he says no . . . we erase and start over."

"How many times has he said yes?" I ask.

Susan bites her lip. "Never."

"You've never saved a single recording?" says Val. "Why not?"

Susan just shrugs her brow. "It's one of the rules. When you're a former addict, you have to have rules. Rituals. In this process, I respect his wishes. And I'm glad I get to hear him, even if I'm the only one."

"But what if the songs are great?" I ask.

"Oh, they are," says Susan, "but that's just it: Eli loves to make music, to feel it, to breathe life into it. But from his point of view, everything that went wrong with Allegiance, and with his own life, happened when the music went from being just a creative expression, just *art*, to a

166

product. Something you sold, something you got *credit* for, something that determined whether you were going to be able to eat the next week, or later, buy as big a mansion as your friends. He thinks it ruins everything. Destroys friendships, lives, but most of all, turns art into dollars. I think he has a point. . . ."

"He does," I agree, thinking of Jon and Caleb fighting over who got noticed more on stage, or the sticky conversations about the Candy Shell advance. Even about finding Eli's songs. Were we looking for art, for a connection, or for the ticket to playing cool shows and getting fans? There's no line between those two things, except the one you make in your head.

"If it were only up to him, we would erase it immediately after we were finished, but I've convinced him to at least take the time between when we see each other to think about it. Never works, though. Songs are what killed him, in a sense. They're also what keep him alive. . . . As long as they're never finished."

The tape machine whirs down and clicks to a stop.

"No. A lot of times we do the same songs from session to session. Eli will track and re-track them, sometimes for years, and then at some point, he stops doing that song, swaps in another. The tape reel is only thirty minutes long."

"How many songs have come and gone in these sessions, over the years?" I ask.

"Twenty?" says Susan. "Fifty? Sometimes there are

snippets. There have been some beautiful ones." There's a note of heartbreak in Susan's voice.

"So then why even record at all?" I ask.

"Because that makes it real. It creates that real performance pressure that only hitting that red record button can make. If the tape's running . . . you play different."

Caleb sighs and gazes darkly down at his father. "Should we go down there?"

"Let's let him play first," says Susan.

"But he should know we're here," says Val.

"I think we should stick to our usual routine. . . ."

I can't hold my silence any longer. I don't want to say the words but I have to:

"He doesn't know we're coming, does he?"

Susan's lips purse.

"Wait, what?" says Caleb.

"You wrote the note on that record," I say. "Not him."

Susan turns to the window, folding her arms. "I tried to copy his writing as best I could, but . . . yes. I've been watching you online, all this time, and . . . Eli doesn't do the internet. Nothing good comes of that for him. Years ago, he told me about those tapes he hid before he 'died.' I could see that you were finding them, and when you got here, I wanted to help you see that through, but by the time you arrived, and I'd already met that Scotland Yard detective, I was paranoid about us being discovered. So yes, I made the note, to get you here safely."

What she's saying makes so much sense, but it's also filling a cold weight in my chest.

"He doesn't know we're here. . . ," Caleb says.

"No," says Susan.

"Are you serious?" Val snaps.

Susan blinks back tears. "Listen: it's not his fault. He wants to hide again, after New York . . . I couldn't let him."

"Well, fuck that," says Val, her face a storm. "It's time to surprise him." She starts toward the door.

"I don't think you should—" Susan says.

But Caleb is following right behind Val. "This is our choice. Not his."

Susan starts to say more but doesn't. She watches them walk through the door.

There's a click from the studio speakers. "Suze?" Eli says over the mic. "Are we ready yet?"

"This isn't going to go well," she says, I guess to me, as she gazes down at him.

"Great." I hurry after Caleb and Val.

1:18 a.m.

We step through the door. Eli peers into the shadows. "Suze?" he says. "What's up . . ."

You can tell even from the way he moves. Quick. Every motion seems sudden, rushed, like he's barely keeping up with each moment. There's an extra shake, a twitch. He

169

blinks harder than you need to, his whole face squinting. His hand rubs up and down the neck of the acoustic guitar, making a tinny, slippery sound on the strings. Tattoos ring his wrists, his fingers. His hair that, from a distance, looked like a fashionable mess, is really just a mess.

Caleb and Val walk side by side. They walk toward their father. They stop at the edge of the light. I step beside Caleb and take his hand.

Eli sees us now. He doesn't speak. His eyes jump from one of us to the next. Linger on me. I'm the one he recognizes. That girl he saw in a New York club.

You can see him working it out. If I'm here, then these two . . .

"Hi, Eli," says Caleb quietly.

Val sniffs hard as tears fall.

"What are . . ." Eli blinks hard, squinting like we're far away even though we're right in front of him. He leans back toward the mic. "Suze? What's happening?"

"It's me," says Caleb. "It's us. Caleb and Val. Your kids."

"Val . . ." Eli turns to take her in fully. He shakes his head like an insect is buzzing around his ears. "Are you Melanie's?"

"And yours," Val says, her voice hitching.

Another moment of silence.

Suddenly Eli laughs and steps forward, wrapping Caleb and Val in a hug. Caleb half returns the gesture. They both seem stunned. "You two . . . I can't believe this! You—you're

170

my kids." Eli holds them for a second, and then pulls back, patting their shoulders. "And you're grown-up, you're . . ." He trails off.

Caleb and Val are left standing there, frozen in place. I see Caleb blinking. Here in the dark studio, it's hard to tell if it's from tears. He looks like he wants to say something, but he must be so overwhelmed. Val stares hard at the floor.

Caleb glances at me. I squeeze his hand, but I have no idea how this conversation goes. There are five feet between them now, after sixteen years and thousands of miles. "The tapes?" I whisper to Caleb.

Caleb nods. "We got your messages," he says to Eli. "We found your tapes. That's how we got to New York, and we all would have been there that night at Ten Below . . . things just got out of control. I'm sorry we missed you. I—"

"Messages?" Eli picks up the acoustic again and sits on the stool. "I . . . couldn't have sent you any messages." He shakes his head. "I don't even have a phone. . . ."

"I mean the letter in Randy's gig bag," says Caleb, and I hear the same uncertainty in his voice that is making my heart pound.

"Then the tape at Canter's," Caleb continues. "The Jazzmaster, Denver . . ."

"Canter's." This makes Eli look up. "Did you see Vic?"

"Well, yeah, we did . . ."

"How is he?"

"Come on, Da—Eli," says Val. "We followed your

171

clues across the country! If it hadn't been for shit getting crazy in New York, we would have been there to meet you. Why are you acting like you have no idea what we're talking about?"

Eli shakes his head. "I just, I um . . ." He looks at the ground, hands tapping the guitar body, like he's rummaging around in his head.

"The notes," says Caleb. "You left one in San Francisco, one in Denver." With each thing he says, his tone falls. "Far comet."

Eli looks up. . . .

His eyes clear, like clouds parting. "Far comet . . ." The words slide quietly over his lips, like he's learning them again. "Oh my God, you mean *those* tapes. . . ." He glances to the ceiling, and finally finds a smile. It's broken and rusted, and gone in a moment, but it's there, a glimpse, the memories somewhere inside, a flash of reflection in the dark waters.

"You left one in the booth at Canter's," says Caleb, "and then the other in the record."

"*It's all about the vinyl,*" says Eli, his words coming back to him. "But that was . . . that was, so long ago."

"Sixteen years," says Caleb.

"I . . ." Eli's head drops. "I never thought . . . I'd . . ."

I wonder if he was about to say that he never thought he'd be *alive* to see those tapes.

We all stand there, breathing carefully.

"But," Eli finally says. "What are you . . . how did you get here?"

"I saw you," I say. "At Ten Below Zero last Friday. You were onstage. You played 'Encore to an Empty Room.'"

Eli looks at me, like I'm a puzzle that he's trying to figure out. It seemed like he recognized me before. But now . . .

"You were waiting for us," I add, "but then Jason showed up . . ."

"Jason," suddenly Eli's tone sours. "Jerrod's son. So that *was* him. I knew I had to run, that it was a trap." He shakes his head. "I never should have trusted Jerrod. They must have finally gotten to him."

I grip Caleb's hand and steady my feet. I feel it in Eli's words, just like a moment ago with Susan. He's going to say more, and I'm not sure we want to hear it.

"I remember you," Eli says to me, "but I didn't know, I . . ." He glances at Caleb and Val. "Jerrod told me we had something to discuss. Something that would change everything. I . . ." Eli's hands flash around in the air as he talks, his fingers flicking on each word. It's like his body is out of phase, the neurons and muscles cross-wired. "He said it was worth the risk. . . . I got to that bar and . . . I only decided to play songs because I was bored. Needed to keep my hands busy with all that temptation around. Liquor, smoke . . ." He rubs his hands together, now, like he's standing around a fire on a freezing night.

"Jerrod didn't tell you why he wanted to meet," I say.

"I knew I shouldn't have listened to him." Eli's voice rises. Focus slipping. "Sixteen years, you know? I've kept out of sight, got all my routines down. Hadn't stepped out of line more than once or twice, hadn't taken any risks. Now . . . my stuff's all in a storage locker, that bastard Kellen is out there somewhere, and . . ."

"Hold on," says Caleb quietly. "You're saying you didn't come to New York to meet us?"

"Jerrod didn't tell me why," Eli repeats. "He's using you guys, isn't he?" Eli starts nodding. "Kellen and Jerrod are using you, of course they are."

"I think Jerrod was just trying to get you there to meet your kids," I say carefully. "I think he was afraid to tell you why you were really coming, because you might . . ." I don't want to say *not show up*, or *run off instead*, because I don't want either of these fears confirmed for Caleb and Val.

But Eli continues like he didn't hear me. "They'd do anything to—Suze?" he calls into the mic, like she's the only thing he's sure of. In a life like Eli's, maybe that really is the case. "Did you check the cameras? Is Kellen out front? This is some kind of trick—"

"We're not a trick!" Val shouts. "We're your children! What the hell?"

Eli recoils, like he's avoiding a fist. His eyes widen for a moment, considering Caleb and Val again almost as if for the first time. . . .

"We're not working with Kellen," says Caleb. "We've been looking for you on our own." He swallows hard. "You have no idea what it took for us to get here."

"Wait, no," Eli says. "I didn't ask you to do anything. I don't mess up people's lives anymore, I don't wreck things. . . ." It sounds like something Eli's said to himself many times. He points at Caleb. "You were never supposed to know about me. . . ." His voice rises. Nearly shouting. "That was the deal! I disappear, make it all go away, and no one ever knows."

"I didn't know!" Caleb shouts back. "Charity and Randy didn't tell me until I turned eighteen, last summer. I was going to *have* to know sooner or later, with the money Jerrod's been giving my mom. Same with Val. Jerrod's been making sure we get your royalties."

"Sure, right, but this wasn't part of the deal," Eli repeats, like the stickier sides of reality don't interest him. "Unknown, that was the promise. I can't let you down if I don't exist."

"But you left those clues, the song tapes!" Caleb says. "Why did you leave that stuff if you didn't ever want us to find it?"

"I . . ." The idea stills him again. "It's not . . ."

"We thought you were leaving us a trail," says Val.

"It wasn't a trail," says Eli. "It was a memory. Back then, I just wanted you to have those last songs so that you could remember me, someday. I thought I'd be gone for

175

real. I never meant for you to drive across the country, or whatever you did. Or to fly here. Kellen probably followed you. That's how he ended up on my doorstep. . . ."

"Wait, hold on." Val uncoils, her venom back. "Don't blame us for this! You're responsible for this, too. Whether you like it or not, you're our dad. Maybe we wouldn't have come here if we'd ever heard from you, *ever* in the last *our-entire-fucking-lives!* Sorry to ruin your little fantasy recording session but this is your life. *We're* a part of your life, whether you like it or not!"

"No, no." He waves a hand at Val like she's started speaking in another language. "I left that life behind, it was best for everyone. . . . You all knew that. You knew . . . You . . ." He shakes his head. Then snaps back up. "Where are the tapes now?"

"Why do you even care?" asks Caleb.

Eli stands. "Do you have them? They need to be destroyed. We'll get a magnet, some water . . ." He puts the guitar on its stand, and starts patting at his shirt as if he might actually have a magnet on him.

"We gave them up," I say. "In order to get the money to fly here."

"Gave them up. Wait, you *sold* the tapes? My last recordings?"

"A minute ago you barely even remembered them," Val mutters.

"There can't be any recordings!" Eli looks pleadingly

up at the ceiling. "Permanence leads to punishment, to pain. Have to *erase* those tapes. Who has them?"

I know what that answer is going to lead to, but I say it anyway. "Candy Shell."

Eli rocks back and forth. "Oh, oh, that's rich." He staggers almost like he's been drinking, and rubs both hands through his hair. "That's perfect. You gave the bastards exactly what they've been after all along. You broke the silence. Ruined it! And now . . . you brought them here hot on your trail, and you want me to be *glad* to see you?" He storms off a few steps into the dark, accidentally kicking the leg of the floor tom as he goes. It topples over with a hollow thunk.

"I did everything you wanted!" he shouts into the dark. Then he whirls back and gazes up at the glass of the control room window. "I got lost! That was my job! To make everyone's lives better by not being. And all I wanted in return was to be invisible. To never be found."

"Eli." Susan steps from the shadows by the door. "Eli, try to calm down. It's not like that."

He glares at her. "*You* did this. You set me up."

"I'm just trying to help," says Susan.

"But I . . ." Caleb is shaking. His eyes are rimmed with tears. So are mine. Everything feels smashed. Shards all around us. "I wanted to know you. You're my dad. I have a band, and music . . ."

"I don't want to know." Eli talks fast. He lunges toward

the sound baffles. Grabs his denim jacket hanging there. "Nope. I don't want to know this. When I know something, when it's mine . . . I break it. Everything I've ever had. That's what happens. You don't want to know me."

He is storming past us.

"Dad . . . ," Val shouts.

"Eli . . . ," Susan calls.

Caleb is silent.

But Eli doesn't stop. "I'm supposed to stay lost!" he shouts at the walls.

And he bangs open the door.

And he is gone.

1:32 a.m.

"Dammit," says Susan. "I'll go get him. Don't leave."

She rushes out.

"Where the hell would we even go?" Val says to the closing door.

I wrap my arms around Caleb. "I'm sorry," I whisper. "I'm so, so sorry."

He laughs lightly, but I can feel his tears on my cheek. "We should have known."

"Do you really think he didn't know we were coming?" Val asks.

Caleb pulls away from me. "For us, everything with the tapes happened last week. For him, it was sixteen years

178

ago." He steps toward the drum set, looking like he might kick over another piece of it. But he stands still.

"Jerrod must have known how fragile he was," I say. "That he'd react like this. I just assumed that seeing Eli in New York meant that he knew about you guys, about us following his trail, but it sounds like he didn't know about any of that."

"Sitting on the plane, I was imaging that he'd been watching us from afar," says Caleb. "That maybe my whole life, he'd had an eye on me. And like, when the news broke, connecting us, and then he saw what gigs we were playing, he put it all together . . . but no." Caleb looks around. "I think he was just lost in his perfect little world."

I don't know that it's perfect. But I don't say that right now.

"Susan was trying," I say instead. "Everyone in Eli's life thought it was right to help us get here, that it wasn't just good for us, it would also be good for him." I glance at the door. "Susan will bring him back. I know she will. He just has to get a grip."

"He's had our whole lives to get a grip," says Val. She starts toward the door.

"Where are you going?" Caleb asks.

She whirls. "I'm going to turn him in," she says. "Because you know what? Eli doesn't get to run again. He doesn't get to be *absent*, to live his dream life recording thirty minutes of music, over and over. It's time for him to

179

take responsibility for who he is." She holds up a business card. "I'm calling Kellen."

"Wait, where did you get that?" Caleb asks.

Val doesn't answer. She's pulling her phone from her pocket. I can see that her fingers are shaking. "He can't walk out on us if we're visiting him behind bars."

"Val, don't," I say, but I can barely muster the energy.

As she stabs at the phone, the tears run down her cheeks.

"Val . . ." Caleb glances at me as he steps toward her. He gently takes her wrist.

She tears her arm away. "Don't!"

But Caleb grabs her arm again. Hard this time. "Stop, don't do it, we have to give him another chance!"

"No!" she shouts, yanking her arm. "Why should we give him another chance? He's just going to fuck us over again! Let go!"

"No." Caleb holds firm, and they are nearly wrestling.

"Guys!" I shout, standing there, useless.

Val lurches away, Caleb falls into her, their heads colliding.

"Give me the phone!" Caleb shouts. He's clawing at it.

She hits him hard across the jaw. A full-on punch. Caleb nearly falls over, but keeps holding on to her.

"Stop it, you guys! Stop!" I run and shove against both of them. It sends them staggering, enough to separate them as they catch their balance. Just that little bit of distance snaps them out of their fury, so misplaced.

Val looks at me, seething, but then at Caleb, then at her phone in her hand. Her eyes are gushing. . . . She slams the phone to the floor. A splintering sound of cracked glass and plastic. "Uhhh!" She hits both her fists against her temples. Drops to the floor, legs crossed, and sobs.

Caleb, breathing hard, walks numbly away into the shadows, staring at the ceiling.

I want to run to him. But I go to Val first. It's for the worst reason: I want Kellen's business card safely confiscated, but, *oh my God, Summer*, what Val needs right now is her family. And if not Caleb, and not her father . . .

Then me.

I sit beside her and rub her back. Her slight frame. The xylophone of her spine. She cries, her breaths hitching, but gets it under control quickly.

She's Val, after all.

"Now what?" she whispers.

"I don't know," I say. The comment makes me glance at my watch. A day and a half until we fly home. I wish it were in a few hours. We all need to get safely away from the Eli wreckage.

"I remember the night I was hanging out in Ithaca," Val says. She raises her head and speaks a little louder, so Caleb can hear. "I saw those tweets from around your birthday. I'd been watching you your whole life, and I knew that right then, you finally knew who your father was. I remember when I was driving across Pennsylvania, rehearsing what I was going to say to you, and I was so excited because we were going to be a family. But then when I got there, I couldn't do it. Came at you through the bass player ad instead, too scared that I'd overwhelm you. But I was afraid of more than that. . . ."

Val rubs her nose hard. "I think, the whole time, what I feared most was this: that the more we learned about our father, the worse it would get. That if we really knew . . . we wouldn't want to know. That actually, our family totally sucks. But even then, I never imagined this."

"Me either," says Caleb. "Can't believe we came all the way here to be yelled at for caring. Please don't call Kellen," he says. "I'd rather have Eli disappear again than have to see him, or hear about him, or anything. I don't want to read the stories about him. Testify about him. Any of it. All that will do is remind me of tonight."

I almost open my mouth and say that it isn't over yet, that there's still a chance things might improve, but I'm not sure they're ready to hear it.

I'm not even sure it's true.

We all stand there, silent. I'm trying to think of what to do next, my exhausted brain trying to find a good option.

"I can't believe we're standing in the spot where the Beatles recorded," Caleb finally says, looking around into the shadows. "Just try to picture that," he says. "They were right here in this exact spot, filling this place with music.

182

Creating those songs, playing them before the world had ever heard them."

Caleb flicks the standby switch on the guitar amp, then sits down on the stool and picks up one of the electric guitars. He strums a chord. The warm, glassy tone fills the room like a bright bubble. He picks up a thick black set of headphones, holds one side to his ear, and taps the microphone in front of him. When he looks back at us, there's a resurgent gleam in his eye.

"Everything's live, ready to go," he says.

Val moves slowly toward the bass. Almost like she can't resist. She picks it up, hits a low note. The room vibrates, recoils, desires more.

We all feel it. Ghosts. Leftover notes still hanging in the air. The energy of a million melodies sung, strings vibrated, drums slapped, all like they want is to form more melodies, more rhythms, to move as one. Like if we play, they will follow.

"Do you think we could figure out how to run the board?" I ask. "That reel of tape is waiting."

Caleb smiles. He glances toward the dark ceiling. Do we dare?

Hell yes.

"Let's go figure it out," says Val.

We hurry up to the control room with a heady mix of excitement and guilt, elves in the workshop. This is probably against the rules. But what hasn't been at this point?

"It looks like she's got it all set up," says Val, surveying the channels. The board is massive, a cityscape of sliding faders and tiny knobs. But only the first ten faders are pushed up.

Caleb peers back into the studio, counting. "Yeah, two drum tracks, two vocals, three guitar inputs, one bass. And these two are room mics, I think. Not sure which track is which, but as we play, you can solo each one quickly with this row of buttons to figure it out."

He and Val give me the quick amateur's guide to the board: how to watch the peak meters to make sure they don't hit the red. The vertical line of three EQ knobs above each fader that control bass, mids, and treble. The channel send knobs that link to sound-sculpting units, like compressors and reverb, the patch bay that I should probably not touch.

"We can't play everything at once," says Caleb, "but we can overdub tracks, so only arm the channels we're actually using, here." He points to orange buttons at the bottom of each track.

There's a small unit that connects the board to the old tape player. The unit is attached to the console by a thin wire. When you hit record and pause, the tape machine whirs and clicks.

"I've got it," I say, which isn't even remotely true, but also I can feel the seconds of our secret session ticking by, so my five-minute introduction to sound engineering will have to do.

Caleb and Val hurry back to the instruments. They grab guitar and bass, slip on headphones. "Summer? You there?" Caleb asks.

It takes me a second to figure out what button lets me talk to them through the skinny microphone beside the board. "Hey," I say. "What do you want to start with?"

"Let's warm up with something we can really nail," says Caleb. "'Catch Me'?"

"Definitely," says Val. "Don't tape this."

"Okay," I say, and hit record as they begin. You'd have to be crazy not to get every second of this moment. Plus, I know Val. First takes are when she's at her most electric, even if she feels like it's when she's most exposed.

They start, and at first it's disorienting to hear the song with only bass and electric guitar. Val counts it off a little slower, which makes it a little more sultry, a little more two-in-the-morning.

Within seconds I realize that while the sound from all the individual microphones are cool and vital, what is the breath, the soul, are these two room microphones. Giant, ancient-looking artifacts on tall stands, each placed in the shadows about ten feet from the action. They are as much about the movement of air as anything, but they also provide the sense of depth, of a real universe. And they make the space for you to enter.

I twist knobs and slide faders like a mad scientist. I find that I like the room mics high, the bass medium, the guitar low . . . Val's vocals slightly wet with reverb while Caleb's are dry, a little quieter so it seems like he's standing behind her . . . I like compressing Val's voice so that her most forceful notes distort. I like turning up the high EQ on Caleb's guitar, turning down the mids on his vocals.

As the tape spins, and Caleb and Val sing and play, I consider that maybe this has been the secret goal of the universe all along. To get us here, to create this moment, through sacrifice and loss and everything else. And it makes you wonder . . . maybe all the pain of tonight, of this week, of this year, has all actually somehow been worth it, purposeful.

Because this is pretty fucking cool.

Also, OH MY GOD I love running the board. I've thought about music and bands my whole life, and I've thought so much these past three years about what makes bands stand out to people in the crowd, what sets them apart, how the little things they do affect the way they move people. But in all that time, I've never seen something like this: this sea of faders and dials in front of me so perfectly represents how I experience music, and how I want to live inside it, twisting its guts and poking at its borders.

A little more bass, a little more Val. Nudge a slider.

A little more thump in that bass drum. Twist a knob on the compressor.

A little less icicle on that guitar, a little more tropical reef. That has something to do with EQ. I can't say that I understand the finer points of kilohertz, but I know now that sound has color.

All of this, the hues, the textures, my fingers flitting around the board, twitching with ecstasy . . . but also we must be cautious. You could do great evil with such power, taking a band's soul and twisting it to fit your agenda. But if you just think of it like a sculptor, revealing the best version of what's already there . . .

Every trip through the song has new possibility, and I'm lost in it. And I am starting to wonder . . .

This is not the sexiest dream, I know.

And I might become a vampire living in these dark studio rooms.

But this is maybe now part of my dream.

They finish "Catch Me." Move on to "On My Sleeve." I pause the tape, start it again just in time to catch Caleb saying, "Okay, we ready?" A little human voice that beckons you.

Halfway through the song, the control room door opens. Susan enters. Followed by Eli, hands in his coat pockets. He glances at me quickly, then at the floor.

They don't speak, hear the song in progress . . . Susan steps behind me and rubs my shoulder.

Eli moves around the board so that he can see through the window. Puts a hand against the glass. In silhouette he is so frail, standing there, slightly hunched. I realize that he will never fully heal from those damaging years, the hurt that he did to himself, but that pain was also the consequence of being an open nerve in a world full of knives.

And yet now he is seeing them, Val and Caleb, beings who share a part of him, good and bad. He's hearing them, and I suppose at this point it is too naive to think that this night can save him, but I find myself thinking at him anyway: *Come on, dammit, feel this. It's not too late.*

The song ends. I pause the tape.

"What do you think we should do next?" Caleb asks me.

Eli turns from the glass. "I'll tell them." He glances at Susan, a look that says *you were right*, that he finally knows it. "I mean . . . I'll ask them." He heads down the stairs.

My pulse races, listening to the hiss of the microphones. They catch the faintest echo of footsteps as Eli approaches.

I can't see him enter the studio, but Val and Caleb do. Neither of them say anything.

Eli steps into the circle of instruments and picks up the acoustic guitar. He checks the tuning. Looks at them. They look at him.

Finally, he says, "Would you guys do a song with me?"

"Sure," says Caleb, his voice heavy with emotion.

"Duh," says Val.

1:55 a.m.

Eli sings over strumming guitar. Sings from beyond the

188

grave, from beneath the Pacific, from across the country, through time:

> *Packing the last of my worries*
> *One last walk on streets I've known forever*
> *Now they're new.*

Caleb and Val play along on electric and bass. Eli nods to Caleb, who joins with a high harmony:

> *I told you I needed new scenery*
> *Before I stopped telling anyone, anything*
> *Anymore.*

Now he turns to Val, and she moves to the mic, standing right beside him. They double the next section, their voices sliding together in knife-edged symmetry:

> *One last time, so we can smile*
> *And give the best we've got, no matter what's been lost*
> *And at what cost no we won't go back . . .*

And then Eli rears back and belts the chorus. It distorts the vocal mic and I rush to lower it just a touch. Through the room mics, he sounds like a pure rock star.

> *And now I'm finding . . . that road home*

Sure I'm finding . . . that home is the moment, not the
destination
Everything you leave behind
It hurts so much to say good-bye
But that's because you know
There's somewhere else you're meant to go.

"Dammit," Susan says behind me, sniffling.

"Yeah." I'm wiping at tears myself as we both watch them play. Eli is smiling as they move into the second verse. He looks so alive, ghost-free, in the moment, and that grin is so much like Caleb's, brighter than he probably even knows.

They play another chorus, and then enter a refrain. Caleb and Val are ready to sing in response to Eli's line:

We can smile . . . one last time
(Abbey Road, I'm finding . . .)
We can smile one last time
(Abbey Road, I'm finding . . .)

They finish, hitting a resounding chord, and all of them freeze, letting it hang, the notes defying time, the song a flock of birds fluttering to the ceiling . . .

Fade into silence.

"I've heard him do that song so many times," says Susan. "Never like that. He told me it was about wanting that moment, like the Beatles had."

190

"What do you mean?"

"When they got together to make *Abbey Road*, they all knew, at least on some level, that it was their last album together, and so a lot of the acrimony fell away. They were able to enjoy themselves, at least somewhat. Eli always wanted that with Allegiance, even though he was the one that made it impossible."

It's silent down in the studio. I don't think any of them know what to do next.

Finally it's Val: "Want to play another one?"

Eli: "Sure."

Caleb: "How about 'Exile'?"

"Nah," Eli says emphatically. "Not mine. Teach me your songs."

Caleb and Val show him one of their first songs, "Knew You Before." They play it slower and with more of an open feel, fitting the acoustic vibe. Caleb tears apart a box of guitar strings and scratches out the lyrics on the white cardboard insides, and they have Eli sing the main chorus.

About two-thirds of the way through, I have a step-out moment where I really consider what we're witnessing here.

"This stuff is so good . . . ," I say. And the wheels in my head are turning. . . . We've spent so long imagining if Dangerheart got the chance to play Eli's lost songs. But this . . . Eli playing Dangerheart's, in father-son-daughter renditions . . . But I tell manager me to shut up, to just be here.

Then a minute later, Susan says, "This is so wonderful. I can't decide if it's perfect or tragic."

"Tragic?" I say. But I know what she means. "He won't really want to erase these, will he?"

Except of course he will. And even if he didn't: What could possibly happen with them? The whole Eli being-not-dead thing is kind of an issue.

"That's always been the only way he can make art feel pure," she says. "He has to create it just for creativity's sake. Erasing it is the only way to ensure that. Even those last few Allegiance songs, before he died, the ones that could have gotten him out of trouble . . ."

"I thought those songs were what he was in trouble for?"

"Well, yes and no," says Susan. "Part of what Kellen and the rest of Allegiance were so mad about was that they were just about to sign a new deal with Candy Shell. *Into the Ever & After* was their last album on their current record deal. The next deal was going to be huge.

"Kellen and those guys were always going to be able to sue Eli for lost tour money and future royalties after he ditched the band, but it would have been for so much less if he'd just delivered those final three songs. That would have technically fulfilled his obligation to the existing contract. To Candy Shell. So many of their legal knives would have been gone. But Eli didn't trust them to do the right thing with the songs. He didn't trust them with his art anymore. He literally couldn't live with the idea."

"Wow."

All this has my brain spinning. Maybe there is something we can do. . . .

I can't be sure, but there's enough of a chance that I take out my phone and switch off airplane mode. As Caleb, Val, and Eli play on, I send a text, and then keep the phone on, hoping for a reply.

When it comes a minute later, I show it to Susan.

(424) 828-3710: Yes. I think I could make that work.

"Is there a way?" I ask her.

Susan nods. "Let me route a few things. I think we can pull this off."

4:53 a.m.

Caleb, Eli, and Val work through six songs. Sketching them out, laying down basic tracks, then going over them to resing harmonies, overdub background vocals. Add guitar parts. Even drums now and then. They bop around in the island of light just creating, at first speaking quietly, but eventually louder, nodding, smiling, even laughing. They never talk about anything other than parts, structure. They speak to each other in song.

When they are finally finished, spent and breathless, it seems like no time at all has passed, and yet I can feel the hours of lost sleep in my shoulders and neck.

They put down their instruments and climb wearily up

to the control room. They are quiet, total exhaustion setting in, I'm sure. They all sit on the couch, the three of them side by side, sipping water, staring off into space.

"Ready?" Susan asks, after a moment.

"Ready," says Eli. This feels like another part of his ritual.

Susan hits play, and we spin through the just-recorded tracks. Twenty-seven minutes of work hewn from three hours of energy. In a hundred different moments, one of us laughs, or shakes our head in admiration at what we are hearing.

There's even one time when Eli says: "I dig the way you drove the compressors on that bass track."

And Susan says: "That was all Summer."

And I sort of supernova inside, while fighting desperately to rein in a goofy grin.

When the songs are done and the tape hisses quietly, silence settles over the room again.

Caleb looks to Val. Val looks to Caleb. Both of them to Eli.

"What do you think"—the slightest pause for Caleb before he can add—"Dad?"

It's obvious what he's asking. Obvious because it's what we're all thinking. We won't be around for the next session. This has to be decided tonight. These recordings are amazing. So amazing that . . .

But Eli slowly stands, stares at the floor. Puts his hands in his pockets.

He glances over at the tape machine. Sighs.

Sixteen years spent fighting his own desires. Sixteen years spent running from who he used to be. I want to ask him who he is now. I wonder if he's asking himself that same question.

Because he could be something new. Right here. This morning. Like in his own song, he could say good-bye with a smile. I should tell him this. But it doesn't feel like quite my place. . . .

He puts out his arms and yanks both his kids up off the couch, pulls them into a clumsy group hug, squinting hard as he does, emotion overwhelming him. Relief? Guilt? Love?

All of the above.

He kisses the top of Val's head. "We'll always have tonight," he says into her hair. Then he pulls away and steps toward the tape machine.

I watch Caleb watching him. He wants to tell him to stop. Wants to grab him, but he doesn't. His eyes find me. I try to send him all the strength I can.

"Dad," he says. "Just this one night . . . this one time. Don't erase it."

Eli pauses. He stands there looking torn, like either choice will kill him. "Tonight meant more to me than you know. And I'm sorry I can't be more for you both. . . ."

195

He takes another step.

"Dad," says Caleb again, his voice rising in urgency.

But I catch his eye and try to somehow send him a telepathic message: *Don't worry. It will be okay.*

Eli reaches the machine, presses buttons. The tape reel begins to spin. Erasing. Releasing this moment, this one night, into its rightful place in the infinite.

"Gotta let it go," says Eli. It sounds like a mantra, one he's intoned a thousand times. Maybe it's how he survives, the only certain thing he's got, and yet he sounds so tragic tonight, like even he knows the cost of the trap that he's in.

The tape whines, until all that's left is blank hiss.

I find myself tearing up. Maybe because I know what's next.

"I should go," Eli says, looking at the clock. "Get moving while it's still dark."

"Where are you staying?" Susan asks.

"I'll let you know," he says. "Was thinking I'd head to Berlin. Just for a while."

He turns to his kids. Both Caleb and Val are trying to find safe spaces to stare into.

"Will we ever see you again?" Caleb asks.

"Maybe," says Eli. It sounds more like *probably not*. "I gotta come up with a new plan."

"Maybe there will be a way to get you back to the States someday," I offer.

"Maybe."

He hugs them both again, wordlessly.

Steps away, closer to the door.

"I was um, I was wrong, before," he says. He shoves his hands in his pockets, his head twitching. Staring into the shadow beside the mixing console. "I *did* ask for this. Not just that summer, with those tapes. But since then, every time I played, alone down there . . . I was asking. To see you. To set things right. But I was wrong about that, too. You're both already right. You did it without me. So I guess . . . I guess I'm just really grateful to know you. You're both so damn special. And you found each other. . . ."

He sighs. "I'm sorry I can't be the dad you both deserve. When you learn so many ways that you *don't* work right, you gotta stick to the few that do. I only know a few ways to make it through the days. The years . . ."

"We could help, Dad," says Val through her tears. "We could."

"Yeah," says Eli, "you probably could. Maybe someday . . . Thanks for tonight." He looks at me, and at Susan. "Thanks for making this real. I—I gotta go."

"Let me know when we'll meet next," Susan says. I can tell she hates this, but she's done the math on Eli. She's seen the equation. She's probably thinking: if she can just get him to show up again, for the next midnight session . . . Then she can work on him some more. He's come this far.

It's a long journey. Maybe there's hope.

"I will," says Eli. "Okay . . ." He looks at Caleb and Val one more time, and there is a hesitation, like the faintest of magnets tugs between them, and my heart freezes because I can imagine him staying, lunging into their arms, making everything whole. . . .

But Eli White turns and walks out the door. Into the London dark. Back beyond the decades and the sea.

5:28 a.m.

Pancakes.

They're really the only solution.

Up all night + life-changing adventure x seminal secret recording / erased tape = Pancakes.

Or eggs Benedict, according to Susan, but that's too adult.

Once we order, I slip my phone off airplane mode and send a text:

Summer: We want to talk. Meet us at the VQ Bloomsbury diner. Now.

I don't wait for a reply.

"Are you sure this will work?" Caleb asks me.

I share a glance with Susan. "I think it will."

Heaping plates of food arrive, a pot of coffee, along with the obligatory because-we-were-up-all-night milk shakes.

I hold Caleb's hand on the vinyl booth between us, my

head occasionally falling to his shoulder. We shovel pan-cakes, mine blueberry, his plain with some creepy English meat on the side.

"I'll let you know when I hear from him," says Susan, breaking the latest long, exhausted silence. "Where he's staying and all that."

"Just tell him," says Val, "that when he wants to get in touch with us, he knows where he can find us."

Caleb agrees.

"What is it like?" Susan asks. She means now. After meeting the man. A question I haven't been able to ask Caleb or Val yet.

"It's quiet," says Val. She taps her head. "Easier, in here."

"Yeah," says Caleb. "I'm not saying this whole thing was the ideal way to meet your long-lost dad, but, after all we went through, it sort of made me ready to deal with who he actually is."

"I hope he can find a way to get better," says Val.

Susan nods. "I've always believed that he will. Some-how. I mean he is better than he was. But I think he can get even further."

The diner door jingles. Caleb and I are facing it. And we freeze.

"He's here," I say.

Kellen McHugh spots us. He unzips his long coat, a high turtleneck beneath. With his clean-shaven head and small glasses, I wonder if he realizes how much he looks like a supervillain. He grabs a chair from the empty table nearby and sidles up at the end of our booth. Pulls his e-cigarette from his pocket. It glows blue as he takes a drag and squints at us.

"Mind if I have a coffee?" he asks, flagging down the waitress without waiting for a reply. "I was surprised to hear from you three. And what a coincidence: the landlady is here, too."

"Nice to see you again," says Susan, her tone saying otherwise.

"I was sorry to lose track of you last night," says Kellen. "It seemed so . . . intentional."

The waitress brings a mug and Kellen helps himself. Drinking his coffee black. Definitely a supervillain.

I just want this to be over as soon as possible.

"We have something for you," I say.

"Is it an address for my cheating, career-ruining, undead band mate?"

I shake my head like he's speaking another language. And yet somewhere inside I register that Kellen's anger and resentment have their place. "I don't know what you mean, but no. I'm talking about the third tape. The reason we came to London. Eli's last song from *Into the Ever & After*."

"That's charming," says Kellen, "but we both know that is not the reason you came to London."

Val shrugs. "What other reason could there be?"

I slip a thumb drive from my sweatshirt pocket and place it on the table. "This is 'Finding Abbey Road.' The only version that exists in this universe."

Kellen eyes the drive. His hand moves up to the table but he's not taking it yet. "And where exactly did you find this?"

"Same as with the others. We followed clues. It doesn't actually matter where we found it. But there it is. Eli White, live from beyond the grave."

Kellen nods and slides the drive over. "I suppose you think that this will actually satisfy me, that I'd really be so gullible as to believe *this* was the point of your trip, the end of the mystery."

"I don't know what to tell you," I say. "That's all there is."

"And that should square things nicely," says Susan.

"As if," says Kellen.

"Actually, think about it," says Susan. "The delivery of this tape, along with the two that they already gave to your associate, signifies that Eli has fulfilled his contract to Candy Shell. He's delivered the rest of the album. Technically, that's all that was ever really required of him."

"I'm not sure I agree with you."

"Of course you could still pursue him," says Susan, "but I don't think it would be in your best interest."

Kellen leans back. "This is weird, because what you're saying sounds like a threat, and I'm pretty sure you're in no position to be threatening me."

"It's not a threat," I say. "It's just what your boss told us."

"My boss."

"Jerrod Fletcher," I say. "You should talk to him. Tell him about the recording you just received. You might find that now that Candy Shell has what they always wanted from Eli, they are most interested in moving on. Not living in the past."

"Also," says Susan, "we've already messaged an identical copy of that song to Mr. Fletcher, so there'd be no point in accidentally losing that drive, or any such thing."

Kellen taps the drive on the linoleum. "I don't know what you guys are up to. . . ."

"We're making things right," says Caleb. "Just like we've done all along. We gave Jason the other two tapes. Then we came here to find the last one. We wanted to hear it first, since it's our dad. You've got everything that belongs to Candy Shell. And you never would have found them without us."

"I think you're forgetting that *you* belong to Candy Shell," says Kellen.

I manage a smile. "We do. Sounds like a win-win for you guys."

Kellen eyes us, glances at the drive. . . . His eyes widen. "My God, you really did see him. He's really alive. . . . How is he?"

202

I squeeze Caleb's hand, and he answers, "He sounds great on the song. That's all we know."

Kellen keeps looking from the drive to us . . . and then he sighs. "Fine. Play it that way. But if this isn't the song . . ."

"It's the song," says Val. "Go listen to it. We'll be right here. Now let us eat breakfast, already."

Kellen stands. He looks around the diner, out the windows . . . like even now, he still hopes to spot Eli hiding in a corner. And I realize something:

He's haunted, too. He's been watching warily for the ghost of Eli White for so much longer than we have. . . . There's probably so much he's wanted to say to Eli, so many years of frustration. I feel bad for him. Sort of. He's never been sensitive enough to what Caleb and Val have been going through. But we've never really considered what this has been like for him.

Kellen leaves without a word. I'm sure he'll be listening to that file before we've finished our food.

And this is what he will hear: Eli White, singing his song, an electric guitar and a bass playing along. Distantly, there are echoes of background harmonies. It almost sounds like a girl and a boy . . . but it's probably just artifact, or tape distortion. It definitely sounds like it was recorded on analog gear, and sometimes that old tape has ghosts.

It won't be enough to be *sure* where that recording came from. A summer, sixteen years ago? Or about three hours ago?

Kellen will probably think the song is great. He'll probably also realize that recording it, along with the other two songs, is going to give him a moment he's wanted for a long time. A chance for Allegiance to get back in the spotlight, to finally benefit from how Eli derailed them. In a way, maybe Kellen and the rest of the band deserve it.

And yet I wonder, too, if a part of him will still miss Eli, miss that amazing band he once had, those times when they were onstage and the center of the universe and making music and feeling so alive and in it. No matter how many tapes Kellen finds, no matter how much money he ever wanted, I wonder if he can ever have that feeling back. He'll always wonder what could have been. And I wonder if that's the loneliest feeling.

6:15 a.m.

Outside the diner, we say good-bye to Susan, hugging as the world wakes around us.

"Be in touch," she says to us.

"I will," I say. "I have more questions for you."

"Another late-night walk should be in order, even it's by phone across the pond."

"Thank you," I say.

She steps away, but pauses.

I feel it, too. The secret of what we just did. The weight of what we're about to try.

"I hope he's not mad," I say to her.

Susan smiles. "I wouldn't mind if he is."

Caleb and Val and I stumble back through the streets, arriving at the hostel as most of the tourists are getting up. The good news is that the dorm rooms are largely empty when we collapse onto our beds. And we sleep. Hard.

2:05 p.m., Friday

There was a day in there, somewhere. We slept, then shambled our way around London some more. We walked Kensington Gardens, saw the Peter Pan statue. In the evening, we took the train up to Oxford to see the Poor Skeletons' next show. They had us on the list. And they let Val and Caleb do a song for their soundcheck, a kind of unscheduled opener. They played a song that they didn't identify to the crowd, except when Val said, "This is for my dad."

When you've never heard a song before, it's pretty hard to catch the exact lyrics. Nobody knew they were hearing the lost final song of Eli White.

And then we were out too late at the after party, and had to drag Val away from the Scottish boy, and we fell asleep on the train, and by that time we were so tired that we didn't even bother to go back to the hostel. At five a.m., we rented bikes from a rack near King's Cross, and rode up and down the Thames, laughing like idiots, like tourists, like Americans, and loving it.

Then back into the Underground.

Then the airport.

Then a plane.

I find myself watching the door. Last stragglers are still boarding. I have watched all morning, on the train, at security, in the terminal. But Kellen McHugh has not shown up. There has been no dramatic moment with Scotland Yard or any such thing.

Which likely means that Jerrod Fletcher kept up his end of the deal.

It is a deal that goes like this: we hand over the final Eli White song. Then Jerrod makes it clear to Kellen that Candy Shell is no longer interested in talk of lawsuits and potential action of any kind in the future against Eli White or his descendants. Jerrod says that at this point, the three lost songs mean that Eli has finally fulfilled his contract. And Kellen and the band can pursue recording those songs, have their re-release, and get as much money out of the ghost of Eli White as they see fit.

Eli is free, at least from one of the shadows of his past.

And Jerrod says that if, sometime in the future, maybe later this year, maybe next, the world hears something that cannot be explained, that goes viral and blows up the internet . . . he won't interfere. It's generous of him.

I'll always wonder if Eli knew. Did he notice that light blinking on Susan's laptop, or did he sense in some way that while we were listening back to the night's session in Abbey Road, she was secretly copying the tracks to her computer?

Maybe. Maybe not.

He would appreciate that before we went to that diner, Susan opened the tracks, and muted Val's and Caleb's vocal channels before she mixed down "Finding Abbey Road" to give to Kellen.

And how will he feel when we execute the next part of our plan? We won't do it until we've given him enough time to hide again. Given his habits, he may never even know it happened. Or maybe it will finally drag him back into the light. Maybe that, and the clearing of the legal air, will make him want to rejoin his family.

Caleb and Val and I don't know, and we don't particularly care. Sitting on the plane, all three seats together this time, we pass earbuds back and forth, listening to the Abbey Road session, letting it transport us back to that night in the dark, to the gothic holy ground of rock legends, where we lost ourselves in music and possibility. Where two generations of rock stars were together for a moment.

The flight attendant announces that the front doors are closed. Cell phones off.

I send a text:

Summer: Our flight is on time. I will come straight home. I know it will be hard. I love you.

After I switch off the phone, I tap my pockets. In one is a drive that holds the backups of the Dangerheart/Eli

Abbey Road sessions. In the other is Susan's card.

Caleb and I rest our heads against each other. We've been mostly silent today, but in constant contact.

And so we must go home. I think we will sleep for most of the flight.

And then this adventure will be done.

And yet still there is that big question:

So, now what, then?

Part 3:
Summer

A Voice from Beyond the Grave

—*posted by ghostofEliWhite on March 25*

This is the sound of your jaw dropping to the floor.

This is the sight of your face melting.

You get my point.

Now get ready.

You may remember last fall when I posted about
the fifteen-year anniversary of Allegiance to North's
unfinished last album, *Into the Ever & After*, released
one year after Eli White's death. You may remember
that then, not long after, we broke the bombshell news
that Eli had a son, Caleb Daniels, living right under our
noses in Mount Hope. You may even remember that
Caleb had a band called Dangerheart and a song that
referenced his dad called "On My Sleeve."

Then, just last month, I reported the hot rumor that
Dangerheart was about to sign with Candy Shell
Records for the kind of son-of-a-rock-legend megadeal
that would send us all scrambling to check our
genealogy.

210

But you may also remember that, mysteriously, Candy Shell and Dangerheart parted ways just a few days later.

And then of course, later that very same week came the earth-shattering news, reported by the corporate mouthpieces over at *Slick* magazine: the lost songs of Eli White had been found. "Exile," "Encore to an Empty Room," and "Finding Abbey Road" . . . Eli's original demos, recorded mere weeks before his apparent suicide, had been discovered, and the remaining members of Allegiance to North would be reuniting to record the songs and release a fully finished version of *Into the Ever & After*, the masterpiece finally complete, all these years later.

So, all of that was just a little bit amazing. . . .
!!!!

When that news broke, many of you wondered if we would ever get to hear those original demos. Candy Shell recently said that they plan to include one or two as bonus tracks on the record.
But many of you also wondered: How could it be that these tapes remained hidden until now? The spokespeople at Candy Shell said they'd unearthed

some old possessions of Eli's and *kapow!* There were these tapes. Like, some ex-groupie discovered a lost trunk of smelly flannels, and suddenly one of modern rock's great mysteries was solved.

Just like that.

Easy.

Or maybe, as many of you have commented, too easy . . .

BECAUSE HOLY NOW THIS:

What you are about to hear cannot be fully explained, and according to the parties involved, won't be fully explained. In fact, it's almost more astonishing that way.

The links below connect to videos posted by Dangerheart just minutes ago. There's no actual footage, just a title that says *"Dangerheart: The Family Sessions."* At first, the audio sounds like live acoustic renditions of songs from Dangerheart's first EP and live sets.

Until you listen closer.

Until you hear the harmonies, the vocal doubling, the personality of some of the guitar playing.

That reedy voice . . .

Friends.
I'm serious.

Just go and listen, and if you don't make the
connection, throw on one of your old Allegiance
records, and imagine that same iconic voice, sixteen
years later.

And then sit back and enjoy the sound of your head
exploding.

What is this? How is it possible?

Dangerheart isn't saying. Probably because they don't
have to.

Once we all hear these, we'll do the commenting for
them. . . .

You bought your tickets months ago.

Marked your calendar.

Sent ecstatic messages to your friends.

Last week you planned who would drive, who would get snacks.

Found that random friend of a friend who could take that one ticket because somebody backed out. You hope they're cool. Or cute. Or at the very least don't mind Red Vines and Red Bull.

This morning you woke up too early, buzzing with excitement, the world electric with humid hazy air, with the complete perfection of possibility. . . .

Only to get in a fight with your parents, maybe because you were amped, or because there was something you said you'd do, something that could never compete for attention when this show has been the only thing that's mattered for weeks.

Or maybe because your parents could sense, from your boundless excitement, how you were no longer theirs.

Even though you always would be.

You drove around town, picking up your friends. You gathered gas money and filled the tank halfway, and someone bought an ill-advised frozen drink that made the car smell like strawberry syrup and suntan lotion . . .

But you hurtled onto the highway, windows down, thrusting into the brilliant midmorning. You drove with the radio blaring the meticulously curated preshow mix that your friend created, the perfect songs that aren't by the bands you're about to see, but tie them to you via a spiderweb of moments and references. Songs that are, as always, as much about where you heard them, and how you felt and who you were with, as they are about the melodies themselves.

You sat through traffic for an hour to get into the parking lot.

You giggled at the stoned kids in the back of the pickup parked beside you, steered clear of the thugs shotgunning beers behind the port-o-potties. You walked at a near-run, sweatshirt around your waist, tapping your pocket and feeling the imprint of your ticket, over and over. You ran, and you laughed . . .

And now here you are. Walking through the gates. In a mass of people. Passing under a sign that reads: *Insanity Tour*. The biggest one of the summer. Fifteen bands, two stages, forty thousand people. Two of the headliners are in your top-five favorite bands ever.

You find a space on the lawn. It was way too expensive to buy seats. Seats are for poseurs and parents.

Falling to the grass, you laugh, and scope out the cuteness around you.

You laugh, and peruse the list of opening acts playing during these early hours.

You get a text from that someone that you are hoping to casually bump into at some point during this long day. They're being evasive. Or coy. Why won't they just bring their friends over and sit here? It's annoying.

Then your friend mentions that he's heard some good buzz about the band going on next over at the second stage. Apparently there was this huge thing about them online, back in the spring. You've never heard of that band, but it's near the spot where they sell the best pretzels. Plus, if you go, you can be coy, too.

You're in the pretzel line when they come on. Actually you are in the middle of paying, but their first chord makes you turn your head. They rock, full-on, a young-looking drummer who's super cute, a fiery girl with a bass slung low, every movement with an edge, a dude standing in back on guitar who looks like he could be one of the other members' uncles. And a singer who is tugging at you, the melody, the words, you're not even deciphering what he's saying yet but there's this thing happening. *Listen*, the frequency of this band is saying.

"It's six seventy-five," the annoyed cashier says again. You didn't even hear her the first time.

But the sound is washing over you and you feel like those chords, those notes, this feeling, it understands you. It's inviting you in. Spend time here. Inhabit this.

Let's go.

Pretzel paid for, you join your friend in the middle of

the crowd. There are maybe two hundred people watching, and you're literally twenty feet from the stage and there is an intimacy, like you're at a private party. You find yourself glancing over your shoulder to see if more people are coming. Because more people should be hearing this band. More people should be experiencing what you are experiencing, and yet, the fact that they're not almost makes it better. Sure, you hope they make it big, but right now, here in the early afternoon beneath a banner for Mountain Dew, this band belongs to a privileged few.

They are *yours*.

Their next song rocks hard, and you and your friend dance. After that comes a slow song that lifts you a few inches off the ground in a levitating swirl. You feel like you are made of lighter air . . . and also really need a bathroom.

But this song . . . this song.

You feel like you've heard it before.

You know you never have.

Feel like you were made for each other.

Do you know right then, that this will be the song, years from now, that you will hear randomly in a dorm room, in a coffee shop, that will rip you from the future and tie you back to this exact moment? Do you feel your future selves stopping by, a blur of you stretching through time?

Despite all of the newness around you, in all of your future selves, something is imprinting inside you about this moment, right here: the sunscreen, the pretzel, all the bodies, the blinding sun at the second stage . . . this band, your friends, and the feeling that you have discovered the very first thing that is yours and yours alone, well, yours and a couple hundred others.

A secret language.

A pure crystal of the hope buried in the mines beneath your skin.

A conduit between you, and future you, and the universe, and . . .

Possibility.

Yours.

Everyone's.

It's over in a heartbeat. Your friend tugs on your arm. But you're not leaving. The band starts their next song, and this band, do they know, can they possibly know what they have done to you? The connection, the purpose, the infinite that they have made? They're probably disappointed. Wishing they were on the main stage. Someday they will be. And until then, you make it your goal to be sure that they know, that everyone knows. In crowds and on sites and on bathroom walls. Send out the signal, and see who hears. Who out there feels this, too? Your people, your tribe, scattered across a crowded planet, connected by a song . . .

No longer alone.

Their short set ends too soon. You linger as the crowd disperses, watching the stage, watching them unplug. You see the singer glance around the lawn, around the stage, and you can tell he's taking it all in. It may not be the main stage, but it is further than most bands ever get. Like he knows it's precious. One bad break, one lost member . . . And you want to run to the stage and tell him don't worry, you got this. You'll be on this stage again, and so much bigger because we need you to.

Maybe you really should run up there and tell him. People should know when the things they do connect . . .

But he's walking offstage. Oh well. You've already found the band online. Liked, followed, friended, subscribed.

Next time.

There has to be a next time.

12:58 p.m.

When Caleb, Val, Randy, and Matt step onstage, I can tell that the first thing they notice is the sea of empty space arcing around behind the crowd. They know the score: it's such a big festival. They are playing with some of the biggest acts there are, and for all the hype that releasing those "family sessions" caused, enough to get a band with barely even an EP to their name to be invited to play the summer's biggest festival, to be one of the thirty bands that *thousands* of bands would kill to be . . .

They are still a new fish in the biggest pond.

There are so many bands to see. It's so early in the

day. . . . And yet still, here they are. So they shake it off and check their instruments, and as they do, they make sure to look at the crowd that *is* there. These are their next new fans. It's Minneapolis: stop six on the Insanity Tour. Ten shows total. Every time, they've gotten about the same size crowd: two hundred, maybe three by the end of the set. They sell the same small pile of records, but the buzz online grows. More mentions, more shares, more people doing the digital equivalent of turning their heads.

Who is this band called Dangerheart? Wait, why have I heard of them?

Here is how the conversation went, somewhere over the North Atlantic, on the way home from London:

SUMMER: Candy Shell will let us go. We'll have to give the money back.

VAL: We don't have the money.

CALEB: I asked Randy. He can loan it to us.

VAL: Okay.

SUMMER: But that leaves you in a bad way, doesn't it. . . .

VAL: I'll be fine.

CALEB: What are you—I mean, what are we going to do?

VAL: I'm going to go see my mom. And we're going to talk like adults. No more running, no more fighting. She's sick. One of us has to do the right thing.

SUMMER: Do you think it will work?

VAL: Eventually. Might be a couple months of acoustic shows for you, brother, but if we can score something big with these recordings, you'd better believe I'm not going to miss it.

CALEB: All right . . . and Jerrod is really going to take Eli's lost songs and let us off the hook?

SUMMER: He said it was enough.

CALEB: What about Jason? Kellen?

SUMMER: Jerrod says we should leave that to him. We got him something none of those guys ever could, and they're going to benefit huge from it.

VAL: So we're free. So, now what, then?

SUMMER (smiles knowingly): Jerrod also says it's okay if we leak the recordings you made with Eli. As long as we don't actually say what they are. Just let the world figure it out.

VAL: And we're sure that's a good idea . . .

SUMMER: The session is amazing. It's so *you*. Like in a real, personal way. And it's your story. Your true story. The heart behind your songs, your past, it's a part of what makes you something the world should know about. And on top of that, the songs are amazing in their own right.

CALEB: (silent)

VAL: The idea that Eli is actually alive . . . people are going to freak.

SUMMER: Yes.

VAL: So what do we do, just watch it blow up and . . . not say anything?

SUMMER: Exactly. We just let it happen. And keep being us.

VAL (thinking): I hate to even wonder this. But . . . is this fair to Eli? I mean, he thinks we erased that tape.

CALEB: We thought he erased himself. Sorry, but, maybe putting these songs out there will force him to face the world again. To get help.

VAL: To be a real dad.

CALEB: I guess, but the point is, it will be up to him. He'll have something to come back to, if he wants it. But we have a right to have a father. He's already a huge shadow over the band. I say we use it. Like Summer said, it's our story.

And so we found a blog to do the release, and we had Matt record drums on the sessions, and then we put them out there. And it really did blow up the scene for a few weeks. Enough that Dangerheart got invited to the Insanity Tour, and got about a thousand management and agent and record label calls. But it also sold a ton of our songs, both the family tracks and the studio versions. Enough that we told all the sharks, *Thanks, we'll let you know.*

But for all that, life didn't change that much for the band. Val was gone for about two months, and then she came back. We practiced, played gigs. We decided not even to try finding a new guitarist while all this crazy hype was going on, so Randy's been filling in.

Somewhere in there, we graduated, had an all-night party, went to each other's family celebrations.

A few more things happened, too.

And now it's summer and Dangerheart is just another band on a festival stage.

The small stage, but the biggest tour.

The small stage, but with no expectations. A modest crowd, but a curious one. Daunting? Yup. But possible, as long as you remember that you are there, you are a part of it. In it.

This is your chance.

What will you do with it?

So they tune and check their vocal mics, nod to one another, and then . . . they rock. Val moves like steel coils and rubber bands, her hair, chartreuse for the summer, slapping back and forth, willing the crowd to move. Matt is head-down and so into it, and my three-minute stint as the drummer makes me appreciate just how dialed in you have to be to drive the drums, arms and legs all doing their own thing, creating the springboard for everything else.

Caleb is Caleb, only better. There's no doubt anymore. He is the son of a rock legend, but he is his own thing, with his own future. Not his father.

But his father is part of him.

The band is getting so tight. They've gotten so good

throughout the spring and into this tour. It hasn't always been easy to tune out the buzz from the Eli sessions, but any other band on our level would kill for this kind of chance. So you take it.

Take the chance. And then just play and play and play.

And even though I've seen this set five other times (and some of these songs how many times at this point?) I still love to hear them, still love to feel them, still love to lose myself in them, and yet still I have my graph-paper notebook out, pen ready, ears perked not just to what is, but to what could be. . . .

And, as they play, I get a little sad. It's hard to be far away from them. It feels different when you're right beside a tiny stage, or right in the front of a Mount Hope High crowd.

It's especially hard when you're watching through a laptop screen.

The set rocks. Even from just the single angle of the live-streaming camera feed, I can see that the crowd has grown from the beginning of the set to the end. I have a note or two. A thought about the middle section of "Catch Me," about the new ending they just wrote for "Starlight" . . .

"Ready, Summer?"

But that will have to wait.

I turn and say, "Just a sec." I type a quick message to Caleb on my phone.

Summer: Another amazing set. Vocals on Transistor = better

than ever. Tempo on Starlight still tricky. Sight of you on stage = still all I need.

Caleb: Thanks. Sight of you not here = bummer.

Summer: I know. Seventeen days!

Caleb: Seventeen days nine hours and 34 minutes!

Summer: xoxoxoxoxxxxo.

On the laptop screen I see Caleb kneeling by his pedal board, texting me with one hand while he unplugs cables with the other. His hair is flopping in his eyes, the perfect curve of his chin beneath that. He's wearing his Poor Skeletons T-shirt, the light brown one that fits him so well, thin muscular arms beneath, and it's annoying that there will be girls there, so much closer to him, probably getting all crushy . . . far more annoying that I can't touch him, hold him . . .

A world away, connected by a satellite . . .

He stands up, throws his guitar case over his shoulder, looks out across the dispersing crowd like a cowboy about to ride to the next town. . . .

And then I close the laptop.

I head out of the lounge and down a quiet hallway, to a door marked "C" with a red light on above it.

"How was the set?" Susan asks me when I walk in.

"Really solid," I say. "By the time they get over here, they should be super tight."

Dangerheart is going on tour in the UK and across Europe with the Poor Skeletons next month, after Insanity

225

is over. The first show is in London.

Where I'll be waiting.

Berwick Street Studios, a sister to the record store, is no Abbey Road, but it is still a real, professional recording space. Susan and her partner started it fifteen years ago, and their goal is not just to record the music of the hottest new up-and-coming bands in the British scene, but to help mold them, shape them, prepare them for a career in music.

I am their first ever production and management intern, paid in room, board, and airfare.

I sit down at the console. I look through a similar rectangle glass window as the one at Abbey Road, only into a much smaller studio, and see the members of My Sith Dilemma. All-girl, three-piece, edgy rock band. Thick eyeliner, torn retro acid-washed jeans, jean jackets and white tank tops.

"Ready for the next take?" I say into the mic.

"Yeah," says Tara, their lead singer, cold-eyed and severe like Val.

"Remember," I say, "on the bridge just—"

"I know," Tara mutters. "Let them in."

Val is actually one of the reasons I feel like I get this band. In my notebook, on the page reserved for Sith notes, is a recurring theme: show us that heart inside. I know that isn't easy for Tara and the band, they're so edgy and aggressive, and yet I feel like if they were willing to show a glimpse of the pain behind it, then they could be having a conversation with so many different people.

They burst into their song, drums slamming, bass tunneling, guitar swirling, vocals attacking.

As they play, my fingers glide over the board, tweaking faders, adjusting knobs, checking tones and levels. Susan and I play with different combinations of microphone volumes on the drums. We talk about whether the guitar stays out of the way of the vocal. We listen and think and lose ourselves and the hours go by.

It's nearly eleven when we finish, and as is our ritual, we stop at the pub just down the block from the studio for a late dinner and a pint. British pubs mostly close by midnight. It all seems so civilized compared to the States. And yes, I realize that I probably sound like the classic teen-studying-abroad cliché right now, but hey, that's what I am! And it's true.

Susan and I talk about My Sith Dilemma for a bit. We both think a song called "Eat Your Pie" is clearly their first single, but the band doesn't agree. It never ends, the struggle to see ourselves from the outside. Susan tells me more stories from the late seventies, when she was working with a band called Halsey's Butterpies, and the crazy tour they had in Italy. She was dating the guitarist at the time. I finally tell her the story of Ethan Myers. It's funny now. Feels like ancient history.

When we're done, we part ways at the Tube station, Susan grabbing a train. I have a fifteen-minute walk in the

London dark, chilled with a light fog, back to the room I'm renting in a flat with two other college-age girls.

I consider the time and do the math in my head, and make a call.

"Hi, Mom," I say, "it's Summer."

"Hey," she says. "Hold on, let me get your dad. . . ."

I huff a little at this to myself. Of course it's nice to talk to them both, but there's something about it that makes the call feel like a big deal, an *event*, and it is those things that remind me that I'm far away. No longer home.

I tell myself that even if I were still in Mount Hope, I'd be leaving in a matter of weeks. This distance would be happening either way. But still, it just emphasizes that I made a choice, to leave them.

Because I got into Stanford . . .

And deferred. Also got into Pomona, and in a late upset, got denied by Colorado College.

It wasn't easy. There was more yelling when I got back from London. Actually, at first there was eerie quiet. I think everyone was just stunned for a couple days. But then the Stanford acceptance came, and I told them what I truly wanted to do.

"Hi, honey," says Dad, picking up the other line. "How's your week been?"

Amazing, magical, a nonstop meteor shower of epiphanies . . . "Really great," I just say. These are still the little lies, by increment, that I hope to someday get past. They should know that I think it's amazing here, and yet I worry that it will hurt them. "We're recording a pretty cool band. Today Susan taught me about limiters. There was math and stuff."

"Get to any new sights in London?" Mom asks. Mom likes the idea of this internship more when she rationalizes that what I really wanted was to spend some time abroad.

I let it slide.

"Been too busy this week," I say, "but Sunday I'm going to go out to the cliffs of Dover with Janice, one of the studio assistants. That should be pretty cool."

There is a moment of silence. A flurry of black taxis roar past me, racing to beat a yellow light. I picture my parents in their quiet house.

"Your registration materials came from Thornton."

The Thornton School of Music at USC is the top sound engineering and music industry program in southern California. They literally fell over themselves to get me. Apparently, "female" is not a box that gets checked super often in their applications.

"How long does that last again?" Mom asks.

Most of our conversations feel like this: businesslike. Like all we have in common anymore is our adherence to the Roman calendar.

"Till December," I say. And I sort of don't breathe because I know what's coming next.

First a pause . . .

Then Dad: "Any idea what you'll do after that?"

I smile and yet I am starting to tear up. "I don't, yet. Don't be disappointed, okay?"

Silence again. It doesn't seem to matter how far I get, we still end up back at this impasse, like we are speaking to one another from opposite sides of a canyon.

Finally, my dad says, "We're not disappointed."

I almost stop him right there. Yes they are. Of course they are.

"We're just worried. That's all."

"Dad . . ." It makes me so mad! Haven't I proved that I'm not a failure, over and over again? "You have to trust me—"

"Honey," says Mom, "we do trust you. That's not it. We just . . . this path you're on. . . . We can't see down it the way you can. The fact that we worry about you isn't a sign that you've failed. It's us. We're rooting for you, but we know it's your choice. I don't know how to explain that we can worry while still having faith."

I wipe at my eyes. "I get that."

Actually, I totally do.

I change the subject, ask about their work, their upcoming cruise, my brother's visit next week. I tell them about Dangerheart coming over and us going on tour, and they listen quietly, Mom offering a *that sounds like an adventure*.

And then I tell them I have to go. I'm at my flat and it's late.

We say good-bye.

I tell them I love them. They say it back. I hang up, but don't go inside just yet. First, I drift in the hollow place that their calls create, a sea of loss, I think, for how it used to be, I don't even know when anymore. Then there's the confusion that comes with these mixed signals, hope and worry, approval and doubt. . . .

It takes a minute or two for my eyes to dry out.

Then a double-decker bus whizzes by in the twilight and I look up and remember that I am in freakin' London. And I remember how. And I remember why.

So, now what, then?

My father asked me, not a year ago.

Now I am living my dream.

And I don't know what comes next.

And I don't know how it will turn out.

But there's an electricity in the unknowing.

In the possibility.

And there is something amazing about that.

Thanks to the fabulous Katherine Tegen and everyone at KT Books and HarperCollins and to Patrick Carman. Thanks to Erica Silverman and Caitlin McDonald at Sterling Lord Literistic, and to my dear, departed agent, George Nicholson, whom I will always miss. Thanks to my friends and family, and to the authors, booksellers, and librarians I am so lucky to know. Finally, a special thanks to all the band mates I've shared stages with for over two decades now. Looking back, every one of those nights was kind of amazing.

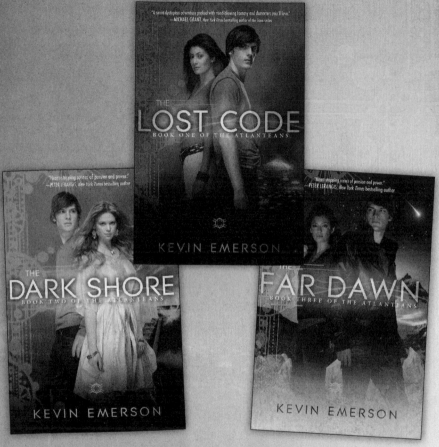